CITY OF ECHOES

AN ANTHOLOGY OF BIRMINGHAM STORIES

EDITED BY:

C.P. GARGHAN

JANE ANDREWS

City of Echoes © 2020

Birmingham Writers' Group

Echoes Past and Present © Jane Andrews

Etaoin Shrdlu © Simon Fairbanks

Second Thoughts © C.P.Garghan

A Smoky Mission © Alison Theresa Gibson

Awake © Kirsty Handley

The Echo Through the Ages © I. Robin Irie

The Colossal Mimic Octopus © Chris Murtagh

The Unwritten Story © R L Parkinson

Reflections © Mohammed Rizwan

Dark Anchor © Sam Spicer

The Crossing Place © Hazel Ward

Cover Design by Chris Murtagh

Published in Great Britain by

Birmingham Writers' Group Press

Birmingham, UK

All Rights Reserved

CONTENTS

FOREWORD i
A SMOKY MISSION 1
ETAOIN SHRDLU 6
THE ECHO THOUGH THE AGES 33
ECHOES PAST AND PRESENT 46
THE COLOSSAL MIMIC OCTOPUS 62
THE CROSSING PLACE 65
SECOND THOUGHTS 83
AWAKE 98
THE UNWRITTEN STORY 113
REFLECTIONS 130
DARK ANCHOR 142
ABOUT THE AUTHORS 159

FOREWORD

Many of us will be familiar with a well-known quotation by the Roman Emperor and Stoic philosopher, Marcus Aurelius: 'What we do now echoes in eternity.' although most of us might be surprised to learn that these words, quoted by the character Maximus in Ridley Scott's film 'Gladiator', were originally written almost two thousand years ago.

The stories in this collection are modern tales which examine the idea of echoes. Take the title, for example: what do we mean by a 'City of Echoes'? The obvious answer would be the physical echoes and reverberations of traffic, or of sounds echoing under bridges or in subways. However, echoes can be more abstract and metaphorical than mere sounds – how often do we talk about the present echoing the past, or a child's actions echoing his or her parents? What happens if we think we're hearing echoes from a past life or lives? It's the stuff fantasy and science fiction is built on.

So, come with us on a journey through assorted stories, set in worlds as diverse as strange fantasy lands, Birmingham's subterranean tunnels and even echoes from future, dystopian worlds. Marvel at the talents of the Colossal Mimic Octopus and recoil in horror from a version of Britain where even sleep is controlled by the government. Follow a disparate group of characters as they circumnavigate the trials and tribulations of modern life, and enjoy spotting the echoes of Greek mythology and classic literature that are seamlessly interwoven into these contemporary tales.

Who knows – you may find that one or more of these stories echoes and resonates with you yourself as you step inside the City of Echoes.

A SMOKY MISSION
by

Alison Theresa Gibson

The floor of the cathedral is dusty, strewn with grass, stripes of manure, and pebbles prised from rubber soles. The sow rolls away from the door, her face towards the back corner where, in days past, the priest would have appeared at the beginning of a service. She snuffles, snorts, grunts her displeasure as one of the teenagers sweeps around her. He's wearing a grey beanie pulled low over his ears, but his eyes are the silver-blue of his whole family. He's a Callaghan, those eyes say. He sweeps the broom closer to the sow, testing how close he can get to the creature before a cloven hoof kicks towards him. He swears and jumps out of the way. The chickens in the rafters rain feathers and dust and droppings and squawk their furious complaints.

Teresa has already collected a wicker basket full of eggs and is now lying on top of the pews stacked against the western wall. Her feet are on the highest point and her face grows redder as the blood pools. Her hand hangs towards the ground but she moves it when the Callaghan boy decides his job is done and kicks the broom so it slides towards the pews and her dangling fingers. She's been told not to get too fond of the Callaghans.

'They don't hang around too long,' her father said once. 'Bad instincts.'

She has good instincts, although her father says she needs to be less sentimental. When Lady Marshall went to check the electricity box outside and never came back,

A Smoky Mission

Teresa had wanted to cry. She hadn't cried, but the fact that she wanted to was too much for her father.

'You done?' she asks the Callaghan boy who has crouched against the wall, his back straight against the cold stones.

'Done enough,' he says. Their voices echo through the empty arches. She lifts her head slightly and feels immediate relief as the blood rolls out. Looking around, she sees Jes sitting on their favourite windowsill, one hand pressed to the purple grapes stencilled in the glass. The adults remember what grapes taste like.

'Jes!' Teresa calls out, and the girl's hand drops off the glass.

'Yeah?'

'Let's go.'

The adults will be back in a couple of hours after a long day defending the city from nightmares worse than those within the city centre. They'll expect a meal, and as it's dangerous to keep food in their huts – even down by St Martin's they might draw unwanted attention – each afternoon the teenagers must forage. Usually, they gather supplies out in the suburbs, but once a month they brave New Street and its promise of fresh meat.

Jes swings her legs around and drops to the floor. The sow grunts. Her belly ripples as her young rearrange themselves inside her and she pushes her spine towards the ceiling for a moment, giving them room, before settling again, her snout in the cathedral's dust. Jes rubs a hand down the animal's flank, and the sow moans. She only allows Jes to touch her and will only eat slops that Jes pours into the make-shift trough by the front door. It's why the Callaghan boy gets stuck sweeping every day.

Teresa says goodbye to the sow because her father's not here to roll his eyes at her superstitions. Jes says goodbye too, but the Callaghan boy just shuffles away, ignoring the beast's presence and the rolling life within her.

The three teenagers swing bags onto their backs, fastening straps around their chests and their hips to prevent anyone, anything, ripping them off. Teresa carries her wicker basket in one hand. They'll be back tomorrow for more cleaning, for more eggs. Once the piglets are born, they'll have to sleep here sometimes, until the creatures are old enough to start the slaughtering. For those few months, they'll be able to avoid the journey to New Street for fresh meat.

Once their bags are strapped on, Teresa raises a hand for silence and slides open the lock on the back door. She oiled it that morning, and it moves silently. They step outside. The pigeons are in twelve barely distinct flocks in the square, each flock fighting only for themselves.

The shadows are long, they're always long, and Teresa leads the others through nooks between buildings. This is the domain of the seagulls, their beaks deformed over decades of disease until now, when they're the only birds who can hook grubs from between stones. They leave the grass to the pigeons and sit in twisted silence as the teenagers pass.

The sound of shuffling and snorting and growling grows as Teresa leads them towards the open space of New Street. Their footsteps slow. The Callaghan boy drops back, his shoulder never leaving the cold stones of the wall as he inches forward. His hands itch at the straps of his bag until Teresa bats them away, worried the dull clinking will attract attention. They keep to the edge, away from the creatures the size of wolves that have taken over the city. Hulking, muscular shoulders roll under thick fur, and teeth glint in the light. The hardest thing is not to make eye contact, but Teresa has trained her eyes to follow the cracks in the cement. Slow step after slow step.

A Smoky Mission

A fight breaks out, and Teresa stops, sweat dampening the hair that hangs around her face, but it's two to one and it's over before it starts. The loser lies bleeding while the other creatures continue their shadowed meanderings. She moves forward again, feeling the heavy heat of the others behind her.

The teenagers reach the open space they need to cross and stop, their breathing loud in their ears. They link arms, and on Teresa's nod they take a step. A cat hisses, fangs snapping, and they freeze until it keeps skulking. Another step. Pause. Another step. The creatures flow around their thighs, barely aware of the slow-moving shadows. Half-way, and the teenagers are exposed by the slanting light that filters through the dense cloud. Teresa can see the man behind the glass on the other side, watching. He nods that they should continue, that he has fresh meat for them, but she knows he won't be coming to their rescue if something happens. If teeth bite into flesh, they'll be left to their fate, nerves on fire and mouths foaming.

The Callaghan boy tightens his grip on Teresa's arm, and she feels his body stiffen a moment before she hears the crackle and notices the unnatural brightness. The fire is just starting, its tongue leaping higher and higher up the tree trunk. A loose wire curls from an abandoned shopfront and lies, now useless, by the quickly engulfed wood. The animals closest to the heat screech and scramble and the teenagers hold each other tighter as the warm bodies rumble around their legs with open mouths and teeth snapping in fright. *Do not frighten the animals* is the first rule they all learned, but there's nothing they can do. Jes makes a noise that sounds like a sob. The man behind the glass turns away, like he doesn't want to see what happens next. The Callaghan boy is shaking so much he makes Teresa's teeth rattle, and she grips his arm tighter, trying to hold him still.

It doesn't work.

She turns her head slightly and catches Jes' eye. They know what they have to do. If they can smell his fear, then it's too late: his adrenalin has betrayed him, seeping out of his skin like a white flag of surrender.

His knees are folding beneath him and the pungent smell of warm urine rises as it soaks into his shoes. Teresa holds Jes' gaze, and the two teenagers stand for one second longer than they should. He is their companion, after all. But her father's voice is in her head whispering *sentimental*, so Teresa gives a slight nod and both girls release their arms. They step backwards, smoothly, like shadows, and fade against the wall.

His shrieks echo down the street as he disappears under the weight of warm, snarling bodies. The two teenagers watch for a long moment, before Teresa tugs lightly on Jes' hand and they take slow steps further up the street to where they can attempt another crossing. The man is watching them again, now that the Callaghan boy's screams have faded. The fire has burnt itself out, the tree nothing but black smoke, and the creatures are calm, for the moment.

The teenagers keep a tight hold on each other and step forward, the warm bodies pressing against their legs, the stench of smoke fading into the night. There are other Callaghan boys with silver-blue eyes, the loss isn't too great, but they'll have to find another one to do the sweeping tomorrow. Tonight, they have one fewer pair of hands to carry supplies back to the huts by St Martin's. In a few years, when there are new teenagers to do the foraging, they'll have one fewer body to defend the city. Her father would be proud that she can think like that, rather than admitting to the sadness that she will never see the Callaghan boy teasing the sow again. In the distance, the flocks of warring pigeons send their calls echoing over the city.

ETAOIN SHRDLU
By

Simon Fairbanks

Chapter 1
Suffolk Street Queensway

Charli could remember her name.

She could remember which city she was in. She could even remember why the city was so deserted –

But that was about it.

What did she do in the world? Did she have family and friends? Where should she be right now?

She found herself under the Suffolk Street Queensway, just outside the Mailbox, gazing up at the colourful lanterns.

She immediately checked her person for clues. That was a good sign. It suggested that whoever she was, she was clever. Charli discovered that she was dressed in a police uniform, complete with truncheon and handcuffs. She searched her jacket pockets for further answers.

All she found was a map. It must be a clue – it even had an X marked upon it – but her head was spinning too much to decipher the shapes and words and colours. She resolved to consult it again when her nausea had passed.

That was another mystery. How did she hit her head in the first place?

Chapter 2
Victoria Square

It was now hours later.

Charli staggered through the empty streets of Birmingham.

Her head still rang painfully but she took the agony as a good sign. It suggested her memory loss was caused by concussion, which in turn meant that it was temporary.

She looked forward to it ending. The deserted city was disorientating enough, without a dizzying head trauma to boot. Charli would never get used to strolling through the centre of the second city, in the middle of the day, without seeing a single –

'Help! Please!'

Charli froze. She was halfway across Victoria Square and dived behind the nearest sphinx statue to hide.

'Don't hurt me!' begged a voice.

Charli took a deep breath, steeled herself, and peeped around the side of the statue. That taught her something else about herself: she was curious.

She witnessed a homeless man, down on his knees, held at the mercy of two sinister figures. Both towered over him, one in front, one behind.

The figure in front looked like an exterminator. He wore an olive-green jumpsuit, with a tank on his back, and a spraying lance in his right hand. His other hand clutched a piece of dog-eared paper, which he shoved towards the homeless man's face.

The exterminator wore a face mask. Not one of the simple cloth masks that had become so ubiquitous since the pandemic. No, this was a full-face respirator, much like a gas mask. It obscured his face, and presumably his speech, which might explain why he wasn't talking. Even so, his meaning was made clear, with the second, third, fourth thrust of the paper.

Read it.

Charli might not have considered the appearance of this exterminator unusual. His attire could simply be related to the coronavirus recovery effort. Perhaps he was a council worker, kitted in overzealous PPE, assigned to spray surfaces with anti-bacterial liquid.

But –

There was something very creepy about the man.

For starters, he was threatening a homeless man, urgently shoving paper into his face. But, creepier than that, was the exterminator's partner, the one standing behind the homeless man.

An executioner.

Charli blinked several times to check it wasn't a delirium brought on by the concussion. But no, her eyes, her brain, seemed to be telling the truth. She was seeing a medieval executioner, kitted out in a black robe, with a hood over his head.

Most alarmingly, he gripped a double-headed axe in both hands. He used the butt of this axe to jab the kneeling homeless man in the back of the head, prompting a fresh cry of pain.

'Ow, okay, okay!' sobbed the man. 'You want me to read this?'

The exterminator answered by shoving the paper forward a fifth time.

'Right, yes, okay.' The poor man tried to focus his rheumy, tear-filled eyes on the paper. His face crumpled into a frown. 'I – I don't understand. Why?'

Another whack from the butt of the axe put an end to that question.

'Okay, sorry!' The man held up both hands in surrender. 'I'll read it.' The man took a deep breath and squinted at the paper. 'Eleven,' he began, in a stammering, snotty voice. The exterminator and executioner leaned in, eagerly. 'Eleven be – ben –' The man continued. 'Eleven bene –'

His shoulders sagged, defeated.

'I can't,' he sobbed. 'I'm sorry. My reading isn't so good. I didn't finish school.'

The exterminator bowed his head in a huff. The executioner slammed the butt of his axe into the ground, frustrated.

'Please,' pleaded their victim. 'I just want to go.'

The two figures exchanged a glance. The executioner indicated his axe. The exterminator nodded.

'Please, no, please, please –'

The executioner circled round to the front of their captive, taking centre stage, and raised his axe in both hands.

'Pleeeease –'

He swung it down onto the ground beside the homeless man. The heavy blade missed his flesh by an inch. The man wailed in fear, now barely making sense, whining in endless vowels.

' – eeeee – eeeeee! –'

The axe came up a second time, struck the ground again, this time on the man's other side. More inhuman screeching.

' – eeeeee!'

The exterminator savoured the man's fear, head raised to the sky, euphoric, breathing in deeply.

Enough was enough.

Charli retrieved the truncheon from her belt. In that moment, she remembered something else about herself too. She was courageous.

'Hey! Get away from him!'

She revealed herself, truncheon raised, and ran at the two bastards. She didn't have a plan. She simply hoped her surprise appearance would be enough to scare them off.

It almost worked.

The two men took a step backwards in shock – but no more than one. Charli's battle charge reached them in seconds, and she had to halt accordingly. Still, she held her ground. She pointed her truncheon at the two men, rapidly shifting its focus between them both.

'Go on,' she cried, desperate. 'Get lost!'

They exchanged another glance, wordlessly trying to decide something. The exterminator tilted his head to one side. The executioner shrugged.

Their agreement made, both turned back to Charli in perfect unison. They marched speedily towards her, stepping in tandem, weapons raised. It didn't look good for Charli, but she was ready to fight.

'Run!' she yelled at the homeless man. He didn't need telling twice. He scarpered, throwing the piece of paper – eleven bene whatever – behind him.

To her attackers, she yelled, 'Come on then!'

The executioner raised his axe –

Could she hear footsteps?

'Away, Echoes. Away!'

Four new figures charged into the fray, bowling into her two attackers. The impact knocked the exterminator and executioner off balance. They crashed into each other and fumbled their weapons.

Her four saviours – two men, two women – regrouped in a protective line, wielding their own weapons, and rushed forward together. They succeeded in driving the two villains backwards towards the top of the fountain steps, where both lost their footing and took a hefty tumble.

Her saviours held their line formation at the top of the steps, allowing Charli to get a good look at them. They were a motley crew. Judging from their clothing, Charli took them to be a doctor, gardener, artist, and biker. But they were organised. They readied their weapons – a variety of curious, exotic blades – in preparation for a reprisal from their fallen foes.

'Charli,' snapped the woman in motorcycle leathers. 'Don't just stand around.'

Charli didn't waste time asking how the biker woman knew her name. She ran to join the battle line, truncheon in hand. She stood next to the biker, only to be snapped at again.

'Wrong formation, Charli,' said the biker, pointing with her dagger. 'Stand by Oscar.'

'What?' said Charli. 'You want me to stand at the other end?'

'Obvi –' The biker paused. 'Wait. What did you say?'

'I asked why you want me on that end.'

'Shush!' hissed the biker, outraged. 'Charli, show caution. You know you can't talk in that way.'

'In *what* way?'

A man's voice interrupted. 'Charli, in position. Now!'

It was the big man at the other end of the line. He wore a white doctor's coat and held a throwing axe. The biker had referred to him as Oscar. He jabbed a finger at the space to his right.

'Okay,' said Charli. She did as she was told – just this once – and completed the line, truncheon raised.

Meanwhile, her two attackers had gathered themselves at the bottom of the fountain steps. They stared up at Charli and her new gang. Or was it her old gang?

Either way –

Five against two, she thought, triumphantly.

Etaoin Shrdlu

The exterminator and executioner looked at each other. They must have agreed to retreat because both turned and walked away. Yet, the exterminator glanced back towards Charli, head tilted in thought.

Charli felt uneasy. A mindless maniac was bad enough, but this one seemed to be thinking, calculating, hatching a plan.

Then they were gone.

'Good riddance,' said the man stood on Oscar's other side. He was dressed for gardening, in waterproofs and wellies, and brandished a sickle-shaped blade.

His words signalled the end of the encounter, and her four saviours lowered their weapons. They all turned to her, with varying looks of concern, annoyance, disappointment.

'Why did you run off, Charli?' demanded Oscar. 'This group only works if it stays as a unit.'

But Charli wasn't listening. The discarded piece of paper caught her eye, fluttering across the ground in a scanty breeze. She had to know.

'Charli, I'm talking to you.'

Instead of answering, Charli held up a silencing finger and went to snatch up the paper. She inspected its contents. The words sent a shiver down her spine.

Eleven benevolent elephants never weathered wetter weather better.

Nonsense?

The two villains wanted the homeless man to read aloud utter nonsense. They wanted it so badly that they were willing to threaten his life with an axe.

'Charli,' said the second woman from the group, the one who Charli assumed was an artist. She wore a long, baggy shirt, stained with a rainbow of paint smudges. She had a kind face, equally smudged, though instead of a paintbrush, she carried a short spear. 'What's going on with you?'

'What is this?' asked Charli, holding up the paper.

Her four saviours stared in bafflement.

'You don't know?' said the artist. 'And you don't know us?'

'I've lost my memory,' she explained. 'I guess I took a fall, because I don't recall amnesia being on the list of coronavirus symptoms. Plus, my headache is excruciating.'

Now, her four saviours looked terrified.

'Will you stop that!' snapped the biker woman.

'Stop what?'

'Talking in that way.'

'What *way*?' shouted Charli. 'Will somebody please explain what is happening?'

'If you do that again –' began the biker, advancing, temper flared.

'Dilta, stop!' shouted Oscar, blocking her approach. He seemed to be the leader. 'Fighting won't do us any good.'

'But –' began Dilta.

'I just want answers,' insisted Charli. 'Who are you? Who am I? Who were they? Why were they making a homeless man read this tongue-twister?'

'There's no time,' said Oscar. The other three winced, recoiled, gasped.

'Oscar, you just said it too,' said Dilta, appalled.

'I know!' he yelled. 'Just this once, we'll use it. If Charli has lost her memory, then it jeopardises the entire strength of our group. We need her with us, otherwise we can't keep those monsters at bay. We have to tell her everything.'

'Finally,' said Charli, relieved.

'But not here. They've figured out something is different about you, Charli. We need to move before they return with bigger numbers.'

'Who?' she said, exasperated. 'Who are they?'

'Echoes.'

'What is that? Like a gang?'

'Oh, god,' said Dilta. 'You truly don't know.'

Charli ignored her. 'Bigger numbers? How big?'

'Big enough,' said Oscar. 'This is an entire city of Echoes.'

Chapter 3
The Palisades

Charli followed the others to the Palisades.

'This will do,' said Oscar, booting open the door of a boarded-up café. 'In here.'

They bundled inside the dusty mausoleum. The décor suggested it was once a vegetarian café. Now, the furniture remained, but the premises had long since been abandoned.

'Victor, watch the door,' said Oscar, to the gardener.

'Yes, boss.'

'India, check for any other ways in.'

'On it,' said the artist, heading for the kitchen.

'Is this your hideout?' asked Charli.

'It is now,' said Dilta, dragging out a chair.

'There's countless places like this across the city,' explained Oscar. 'Casualties of the imposed lockdown. Mostly niche places who used to survive month to month. They were the first businesses to shut once they were starved of customers.'

'The age of COVID,' muttered Dilta, resting her boots on the table.

'Which is how our story begins,' added Oscar.

'Go on,' said Charli, folding her arms.

'You might want to sit down for this.'

'Just talk.'

'Suit yourself,' sighed Oscar, taking a seat himself. 'Well, COVID happened. Lockdown came into force. The city was abandoned overnight. A silence reigned like never before. No words, no conversations, no announcements. Just silence.'

'And then what?' asked Charli. 'People with a fetish for tongue-twisters took over the city?'

'They're not people,' said Dilta, darkly.

'What do you mean?'

'It's tricky to explain,' said Oscar. He paused, thinking. 'Do you know the most commonly used letter in the English alphabet?'

Charli sighed. 'I'm not interested in any more riddles. Eleven benevolent elephants was the last straw.'

'Humour him,' said India, softly, returning from her recce. 'No other ways in,' she added to Oscar, who nodded.

'Just tell me,' said Charli.

'Etaoin shrdlu,' said Victor, still keeping watch at the door.

'Pardon?' said Charli.

'The twelve most commonly-used letters, in order,' translated Oscar. 'E is used far more than any other letter. Samuel Morse discovered that when he created Morse code. Peter Norvig discovered the same thing, two centuries later.'

'Who?'

'The Google guy,' said Dilta.

Oscar continued. 'The letter E likes to be used. Over millennia, it has grown accustomed to hearing its name spoken, seeing its name in publications. The more it was used, the more it was satisfied, nourished, placated.'

Charli stared.

'Then silence descended on our city. The letter E ceased to be used. Suddenly, without warning, the most adopted and powerful letter knew neglect for the first time. It finally understood hunger.'

'Okay,' said Charli, slowly taking a seat.

'The letter E was desperate, starving, but it wasn't weak. It had plenty of power after being spoken so frequently over the years. It simply never had cause to use that power before. But the time had come. The letter E became manifest. It assumed physical form.'

Charli's head spun. Not because of her concussion, which was easing, and not because Oscar was describing a bonkers concept with complete conviction. No, her head spun because part of her knew it was the truth. Her recovering memory was giving her the thumbs-up, greenlighting what should have been a ridiculous fantasy.

An intangible letter has sentience and appetite and now a form. Sure.

Instead of challenging Oscar's story, she said, 'Physical form?'

'Well, forms, plural,' corrected Dilta.

'Like exterminators and executioners?'

'That's right,' said Oscar.

'And elves and emperors and ecclesiarchs,' added India.

'It picks forms that reflect its letter,' said Oscar. 'They always begin with E, and contain multiple uses of E. Perhaps that reinforces its power.'

'But why do you call them Echoes?' asked Charli.

'The phonetic alphabet,' said Dilta, with a shrug. 'E is Echo. We needed a name for them, and that made as much sense as any.'

'But what do they want?'

'Sustenance,' said Oscar. 'They want to be spoken again.'

Charli understood. 'Eleven benevolent elephants.'

'Exactly. The Echoes prey on anyone still passing through the city.'

'But the city is deserted.'

'There are still people.'

'What people?'

'People not following lockdown. Homeless people. Key workers. Covidiots.'

'And they force them to speak the letter E?'

'Yes. Usually as part of a word, or phrase. And if a person can't, or won't, read the paper given to them – Well, you saw what happens next. The Echoes torment and torture them. They're getting pretty good at it, too.'

Dilta grunted. 'Lots of E sounds in squeals and shrieks and pleas for mercy.'

'So why the tongue twisters?' asked Charli.

'Tastier, more filling, who knows,' said Oscar.

'There is strength in words,' said Victor, sagely. His eyes never left the slats through which they peered.

'And what if the person complies?' asked Charli. 'What if they read the tongue-twister for the Echoes?'

'Then the Echoes force the person to keep reading until they collapse from exhaustion or dehydration.'

'Or lose their voice,' added India.

'Or their mind,' said Dilta.

Oscar nodded, heavily. 'We once found a person who the Echoes had held hostage for days. The Echoes have no other place to be. It's hard to drag them away from the buffet table.'

'Monsters,' said India.

Charli gripped the arms of her chair to steady herself. 'And what? Your gang rallies together to fight the Echoes?'

'*Our* gang,' said Oscar. 'You are one of us.'

'What makes us so special?'

'Isn't it obvious?' asked Dilta, frowning.

'Amnesia, remember?' said Charli, pointing to her head.

Dilta scoffed. 'You don't need your memory to work this one out.'

'Listen, you –'

India intervened, calmly. 'Charli, think about our names. What are they?'

Charli folded her arms, impatient, but answered all the same. 'Oscar, Victor, India and Dilta.'

'It's actually Delta,' said India. 'But we pronounce it Dilta.'

'No sense in feeding the Echoes by speaking the letter E,' explained Oscar.

The penny dropped. 'That's why you were shouting at me in Victoria Square. You said I was talking in a certain way. I was using the letter E. The rest of you were avoiding it.'

'That's right.'

'And now we're all doing it,' muttered Dilta. 'Thanks Oscar.'

'You try explaining this without the full alphabet,' said Oscar, hotly.

'We dropped the E from your name too, Charli,' said India, softly. They all turned to Charli – except Victor, still on lookout – to see how she would react.

'See the pattern, finally?' asked Dilta.

'The phonetic alphabet,' said Charli, standing up. 'We're letters too.'

Dilta did a mocking slow clap. 'Well done.'

'Yes, we're letters,' said Oscar.

'But –' Charli shook her head. 'No, I'm not a letter. I'm a police officer. Look, I have a police jacket, a truncheon, handcuffs.'

'No,' said India, smiling. 'You are a constable, with a coat, club, and cuffs.'

Oscar nodded. 'Much like the Echoes, we pick forms that reflect our letter.'

'But you're a doctor,' protested Charli, pointing at his white coat. 'That doesn't begin with O.'

'I'm an oncologist.'

'Oh.' Charli frowned. 'But what about the rest of you? A gardener, artist and biker?'

'Viticulturist,' said Victor.

'Impressionist,' said India.

'Deliveroo driver,' said Dilta.

Charli rubbed her head, processing the information. 'But your weapons –'

'I carry an onzil,' said Oscar, holding up his throwing axe. 'Victor wields a vechevoral, India uses an ikiwa, and Dilta has a dirk.'

'And I have a club?'

'Yes. Like I said, we pick forms that stay close to our letter. Consider yourself. What have you learnt about your persona since waking up?'

Charli recalled her discoveries from earlier that morning. 'I'm clever, curious and courageous,' she said quietly.

'And cocky,' said Dilta.

But Charli wasn't listening. What other C-words were part of her nature? She remembered the map in her pocket. Cartography, perhaps?

Oscar continued. 'But even with these forms, we're nowhere near as strong as the Echoes. We can't manifest multiple times, in multiple forms. We just have one form each, and we can only form people.'

Etaoin Shrdlu

'Our letters aren't used as much as E,' said India, sadly.

'Etaoin shrdlu,' repeated Victor.

'But that is starting to change,' said Oscar.

Charli frowned. 'You're not forcing your own tongue-twisters on people, are you?'

'Goodness no. But in recent months, our five letters are being used more and more frequently, across the entire planet. It has given us just enough strength to manifest, allowing us to make a stand against the Echoes.'

'Why our letters?' asked Charli. 'Why now?'

'Charlie, Oscar, Victor, India, Delta.'

Her eyes opened wide. 'COVID?'

'Precisely. With each passing day, the word COVID is mentioned in more conversations, more broadcasts, more newspapers, and more webpages. We are growing stronger.'

Charli dropped back into her chair, trying to process the information. 'But you said it yourself. This is an entire city of Echoes. How can five people take on that many Echoes?'

'There is strength in words,' repeated Victor.

Oscar nodded. 'When the five of us line up in the correct order, we spell out COVID, and it gives the Echoes pause for thought. We might be weak as individual letters, but together as that word, which is being used countless times a day around the world, we have enough power to scare off the Echoes.'

'More often than not,' amended Dilta.

'That's why we need you, Charli,' said India. 'That's why we were so hurt when you ran away.'

'I wasn't hurt,' spat Dilta. 'I was pissed off. What were you thinking?'

Charli had grown tired of Dilta's snarky comments. 'All right, settle down. I don't remember running away.'

'Settle down?' Dilta jumped to her feet, glaring.

'Enough, enough,' said Oscar. 'It's in the past. Charli is back. That's all that matters. And, Charli, please, don't leave us again. Our advantage is slim at best. Their fear of us barely holds, and it would vanish altogether without you to complete our line-up.'

'Okay, I won't run off. I'm with you. Relax.'

Oscar fretted. 'I'm already worried about how that exterminator was looking at you. If they suspect we have a crack in our gang, they'll regain their confidence. The Echoes will regroup and throw everything at us. Exoskeletons, ectoparasites, exorcists –'

'Elephant!' cried Victor.

'I'm never seen an elephant before,' said India.

'You're about to! Get against the walls!'

Victor leapt away from the door –

BOOM.

The café front imploded. Chunks of wood and shards of glass showered towards them, swiftly followed by the twin tusks of an enormous elephant, which hurtled into the café.

Charli dived to the side. She hit the ground, head-first, and instinctively rolled away, only narrowly avoiding her skull being crushed beneath stampeding feet.

The elephant swung its trunk, stomped its feet, butted its bulbous head around the room. It obliterated the counter, furniture, ceiling panels, artwork – all the while its tusks were seeking the five occupants of the café.

'Well, this fucker isn't benevolent,' shouted Dilta, somewhere to Charli's side. She ducked a swipe of the beast's trunk.

'At least there isn't eleven of them,' replied Charli, finding her feet. 'Yet.'

Thankfully, the Echo had overestimated the size of the café. Its elephant form was finding it hard to move around, hence all of its wild thrashing. This allowed the five of them to scurry out of the broken café window, and escape with their midriffs free of any tusk punctures.

But once outside, they skidded to a halt. A herd of elephants awaited them.

'Ah,' said Charli. 'Apparently, there *are* eleven of them.'

'At least,' said Dilta.

The frontmost elephant stomped a foot and let out an ear-splitting trumpet. The sound was returned by the elephant in the café. It had found its way free of the furniture, and now loomed behind them.

'What do we do, Oscar?' cried India.

'Um, line-up?' came his reply.

'No!' said Charli, retrieving the map from her pocket. 'Follow me.'

'Running off again?' asked Dilta.

'Trust me,' said Charli.

'Why should we?'

'I'm the leader, right?' said Charli. 'Me, not Oscar. That last jolt to the head brought back some more memories. You followed me before; follow me again.'

'Where to?'

'Not sure.' She waved the map. 'X marks the spot.'

Chapter 4
Centenary Square

The group sped across the city, following Charli at every turn.

The elephants stampeded after them. They would have crushed the five of them into the ground had it not been for Charli's constant zigging and zagging.

Still, they showed no sign of giving up. It was only when they darted into Needless Alley, a famously narrow street, that they managed to lose them. The first elephant charged in headfirst, stupidly wedging its bulk into the mouth of the alleyway. That stopped any other Echoes following, whether elephantine or otherwise.

'That'll hold them,' said Oscar. 'Can we stop for a rest now?'

Charli shook her head. 'No, there'll be more on the way. Listen.'

'Are those wings?' asked India.

'Eagles, I'm guessing,' said Charli.

'No,' said Victor. 'They sound bigger.'

'Then all the more reason to keep moving. This way.'

'Yes, Chief,' grumbled Dilta.

They ran on and on, terrified, hounded, exhausted, but Charli didn't let them rest until they reached the X on her map.

'Here,' said Charli, coming to a halt. 'This is the place.'

The others skidded to a standstill beside her, catching their breath, hands on hips.

'Why here?' gasped Oscar, looking around.

'X marks the spot,' said Charli, consulting her map yet again.

Dilta shook her head. 'This is ridiculous. You have amnesia. That map could have been planted on you by the Echoes for all you know. This could be a trap.'

'No, I think this is my map.'

'Why?'

'I'm the letter C, right?'

'Yes.'

'I'm a cop, and clever, courageous, curious. It stands to reason that I'm a cartographer too.'

'A what?'

'A map specialist. And I'm pretty sure the X marked on the map is my own. I recognise my handwriting.'

'It's one letter, Charli,' said Oscar. 'How can you be sure?'

'Calligraphy,' said Charli, with a grin. 'Another of my specialities.'

Dilta rolled her eyes.

Charli paced, thinking. 'I reckon I was making my way here when I had my head injury. I woke under the Suffolk Street Queensway, down by the Mailbox. I think I was walking up the Queensway to this location when one of the Echoes knocked me over the railing.'

'But what's so important about this place?' asked Oscar.

'I don't know,' said Charli.

The X on the map had led them to the Hall of Memory, the World War One memorial in Centenary Square. They considered the memorial now. It was now late in the day, past dusk, and the automatic lights had clicked on inside the domed, stone building. The doors stood open. Nobody had thought to lock the memorial before lockdown had been enforced.

'Well, that's just great, isn't it?' snapped Dilta.

But Charli wasn't giving up. She pointed at the boards erected around the memorial. 'What are these?'

'It's an outdoor exhibition,' explained India. 'Marking one hundred years since the World War One armistice. It was a big deal two years ago, so the city kept them up.'

Each board showed different photography of the war effort around Birmingham and how citizens did their bit to help.

'There must be a reason why I wanted us to gather here,' said Charli, searching the boards for answers.

'I thought you had all the answers,' said Dilta, with venom. 'C for clever, right?'

'I am clever,' protested Charli. 'I'm also confused, so just give me a minute.'

She considered the Hall of Memory. The inner walls were engraved with the dates when people had died in the war. Countless occurrences of the years between 1914 and 1918.

'Tell me about this place,' said Charli. 'Everything. Anything. It could all help.'

'Okay,' said Oscar. 'This is the Hall of Memory. It opened a year after the war in 1919 to commemorate the fallen heroes of Birmingham.'

'What's that over there?' she asked.

'That's the REP,' said India. 'A theatre.'

'Why do they have so many eyeballs in their windows?'

'Big Brother. They were showing a stage production of Nineteen Eighty-Four by George Orwell before the lockdown.'

'Okay, and what's that?'

'Symphony Hall,' answered Victor. 'They stage classical concerts. Mozart's Symphony No.19, most recently, I believe.'

'And that?'

'That's a tram stop,' said Dilta. 'Nothing exciting.'

Charli stared at the tram stop, then her eyes widened in delight. 'Ah!' she cried. 'Ah, yes!'

'What? What is it?' chorused the rest.

Charli turned to the outdoor exhibition boards. She ran a quick loop around the Hall of Memory, counting the boards, and returned to the others with a grin.

'Yes, yes, yes! I've got it!'

'Got what, Charli?' asked Oscar.

'What date is it today?' she answered.

'Well, tomorrow is the Summer Solstice,' said Victor.

'Are you sure?'

'Yes, it's a Norse celebration. I know about Viking things. Part of being letter V.'

'Good, so that makes today – Yes!'

'Charli,' said Dilta, grabbing her shoulders. 'Explain.'

Charli smiled. 'We're waiting for someone.'

'You're damn right. A whole bloody herd of elephants.'

'No, not an Echo,' laughed Charli. 'A new friend. An ally.'

Oscar looked at the map still scrunched in Charli's hand. His eyebrows rose. 'X doesn't mark the spot,' he said, realisation dawning. 'X is who we're waiting for. The letter X.'

'Is that true, Charli?' asked India.

'Not quite.'

'Then which letter?'

'It's not a letter. It's a –'

The lights in the Hall of Memory blinkered out. The five of them had been gathered in the gaping yellow light of its open doors, but now they were left in darkness.

'What now?' said Oscar.

They looked up to see a swarm of eels slithering over the domed roof, sparking with electricity.

'Electric eels,' said Victor. 'The Echoes are here.'

More shapes appeared, emerging from behind the exhibition boards. Charli saw exterminators and executioners and electrocutioners. Behind them, the hulking shadows of elephants slowly approached over the bridge, ridden by environmentalists and entrepreneurs and entertainers. These beasts were flanked by eerie ewes and eccentric electro-violinists and elegiac equestrians on horseback, whilst eagles wheeled overhead in an endless cyclone.

'Now what?' asked Dilta.

'Line up!' shouted Oscar, as always. When the others were too frozen to move, he started cajoling them into position, spelling out their usual word. 'Hold up your weapons,' he ordered.

'It's a little late for that,' boomed a voice.

'Oh no,' said Oscar, weakly.

Charli could barely believe her eyes. A winged figure lowered himself down through the maelstrom of eagles. He stopped several feet above the ground, looking down on them, kept aloft by casual sweeps of his vast white wings.

'We're done being spooked by you,' he said, triumphantly.

'Is that an angel?' whispered Charli.

'Ezekiel,' said Oscar. 'Their leader.'

'Good.' Louder, she said, 'Done being spooked by us? Is that why you brought the cavalry?'

Ezekiel spread his arms, indicating his full army. 'Everyone. Everything.' He gave a smug grin. 'You know how we like the letter E.'

'Bring it on.'

'You said that last time, Charli,' laughed Ezekiel. 'And that encounter ended with me throwing you off the Queensway.'

'That was you?'

'I'd hoped that fall would knock some sense into you.'

'No such luck. I'm a letter C. Constant, ceaseless, committed to my cause.'

'I can think of another C-word to describe you.'

'We're not afraid of you,' said Dilta. 'You're just a letter. We're an entire word.'

'Not afraid?' the angel grinned, showing all of his teeth. 'We'll see about that.'

Ezekiel blew a horn. The note carried long and low. It was answered immediately. A deep rumble shook the very ground on which they stood. A new shape came lumbering out of the shadows, much bigger than the elephants, coated in jagged armour. Ezekiel took a seat on top of this new behemoth.

'Is that a dinosaur?' asked Charli.

'A euoplocephalus,' confirmed Dilta.

'How do you know that?'

'Dinosaurs,' she shrugged. 'Part of being letter D.'

Ezekiel patted his new steed. The creature pawed the ground and swished its armoured tail. It swung a wrecking ball crafted from solid bone.

'Um, Charli,' whispered India. 'If this new friend of yours is going to make an appearance, now would be a really good time.'

'Any last words?' demanded Ezekiel, from atop his dinosaur.

'Just one,' said Charli.

'Ah, yes, COVID. That's not going to scare us today.'

'There's strength in words,' said Oscar.

'There's also strength in numbers,' said Ezekiel, indicating his force of Echoes.

'I couldn't agree more,' said Charli.

'Well, there's only five of you,' said Ezekiel, flatly.

'Soon to be six,' said Oscar. 'Right, Charli?'

'Nineteen.'

'Huh?'

Charli smiled. 'There's nineteen exhibition boards. That tram stop is number nineteen. The number nineteen is engraved on the Hall of Memory countless times, which was also built in 1919. The REP was staging a production of Nineteen Eighty-Four before it shut down. Symphony Hall was showing Mozart's Symphony No.19. Oh, and tomorrow is the Summer Solstice, which makes today – Anyone?'

'The nineteenth of June,' said Dilta, slowly.

'Correct.'

'What's your point?' said Ezekiel, eyes narrowing.

'All this chatter about nineteen in this one tiny part of Birmingham,' said Charli. 'Our friend's ears must be burning.'

The lights in the Hall of Memory flicked on.

Their group of five were bathed in yellow light once more.

And a young soldier strolled out of the Hall of Memory. The youth was dressed for the trenches of World War One, though he had the nonchalant stroll of a student with all the time in the world. He took his place beside Dilta.

'Hey, what did I miss?' he asked, with a casual tip of his Brodie helmet.

Dilta stared at the boy, then looked to Charli. 'This kid? This kid is going to help us defeat the Echoes?' She turned to him. 'What are you, twelve?'

'Nineteen.'

'Still too young to fight. Who are you?'

The boy smiled. 'I told you. I'm Nineteen.'

Dilta turned to Charli. The others did too. She smiled.

'What is happening?' said Ezekiel, feathers bristling.

Charli laughed. 'You said it, Ezekiel. There's strength in numbers. Meet our newest member. Nineteen.'

Ezekiel floundered, fluttering in agitation. Even his dinosaur edged backwards.

'COVID-19,' gulped the angel.

'That's right,' said Charli. 'Because it's not just our five letters appearing over and over again in conversation, print, webpages. There are five letters *and a number*. Now, our line-up is finally complete. COVID-19.'

'Oh no.'

'Ready?' Charli asked her associates.

Together, the letters and their newest recruit gave their agreement. They assumed their battle stances, raised their weapons, and fixed their eyes on the Echoes before them. Charli felt her head clear for the first time that day. She twirled the club in her hand and discovered a strength that she had never known before.

'Hey, Ezekiel, I've got another C-word for you.'

'Eh?' he said, fluttering backwards.

Charli grinned. 'CHARGE!'

Chapter 5
New Street

Charli found Oscar sitting on a bench, admiring the bustling shopfronts of New Street.

'The city is back to normal again,' said Oscar, pleased.

'Is that right?' said Charli, taking a seat.

'Of course,' he said. 'The lockdown has lifted, the city is open again, and the streets are full once more.'

'No more silence?'

'Exactly.' Oscar reclined into the bench, happily. 'Conversation has resumed. It's been enough to satisfy the Echoes and send them back into the ether.'

Charli watched the hubbub of people scurrying along the street. They juggled bags and coffee cups and phones, busily zipping in and out of shops and restaurants. It almost looked familiar. Almost.

'You call this normal?' she asked.

'Looks like the same old New Street to me.'

'Looks can be deceptive. Things aren't the same. They will never be the same again. There are echoes of the virus everywhere.'

'Echoes?'

'For want of a better word.'

'What do you mean?'

'Look closer. People are still wearing masks. Those haven't been mandatory for months. The same goes for social distancing. It's not required anymore but nobody is getting too close to each other.'

'Force of habit, perhaps?'

'Or just paranoia? Distrust? Every so often, somewhere lets their guard down, gets too close to a stranger in the street, and then you see them realise. They recoil, almost in disgust.'

'I don't think –'

'And there!' Charli pointed. 'Look, that person just rubbed on some hand gel after touching that shop door. She won't be the only person today. It's always done discreetly, even shamefully, but the muscle memory is there, the sense of uncleanliness until the gel is applied.

'And don't ignore all the collapsed businesses that are dotted along the high street, now boarded up, or whitewashed, or under new ownership.

'I'm telling you, coronavirus left behind endless echoes, shadows, memories, hangovers, whatever you want to call them. And people are still talking about the virus.'

'How do you know?'

'Because look how strong we are,' said a third voice, joining them on the bench. Oscar gave a yelp.

'Charli?' he asked, looking between the new arrival and his previous bench-mate. 'Charli?'

'Yes, there are two of me now,' said the first Charli.

'And I managed to change shape last night,' said the second Charli. 'Just like the Echoes could. We're getting stronger, Oscar.'

'We are?'

'Of course. The word COVID-19 is being spoken more than ever before, despite the lockdown ending. That increases our ability. In time, we might get accustomed to having all that power.'

'Careful,' said Oscar. 'You don't want to become like the Echoes.'

'That is my fear,' said Charli, gravely. 'If COVID-19 ever goes away, finally fades out of the lexicon, then it will be the six of us who grow hungry. We will become the monsters, desperate to be spoken again.'

'Next time, it might be the Echoes who have to stop us,' said the second Charli.

Charli, Oscar and Charli sat in silence, considering the thriving crowds of New Street.

'One way or another,' said Charli. 'This will always be a city of echoes.'

THE ECHO THOUGH THE AGES
By

I Robin Irie

The deeds of the great shall echo through time to

touch the lives of all in the great circle of life.

- from The Lukasa of Kings

The midday heat pressed down on Mbala, increasing his sense of foreboding. He was not ready; he knew that. Unstoppering a jar, he drank deeply of the cool water and looked out to where the city broke the line where the cloudless sky met the desert sand.

'It's time, nana,' said Wole at his back.

Slowly, Mbala replaced the stopper in the jar; not because he was being careful, but he feared dropping it in the sand. He turned to face his companions. Father, he thought, I needed more time. His guards - twenty strong sat on their heels, spears held upright. He met the eyes of Wole and the other two members of The Council of The Wise – all old men – and not for the first time, he felt weighed and measured. What name would they give him? His own father was commemorated as Akola the Lion; a fitting name for his end. He died a half cycle ago, a glorious death that would make its way into the stories. He had managed to kill ten Nabingis before ramming a spear into their king's heart. It was a cowardly arrow that felled him.

Mbala expected that some Nabingi boy was now getting used to being king with no purpose but to carry on the war that had been fought before Mbala was born. Maybe he was big and strong, and good with the spear or axe.

'You go as you came into the world,' said Wole.

Mbala stretched both arms to the side and his body servant rose and took the jar from his hand. No, he would not compare himself with his father, thought Mbala as the body servant removed his clothes, leaving him naked. Mbala the Cripple? He was good with a spear, maybe better than most, but his left hand was not strong enough to hold a shield. Mbala the Unworthy? Maybe. It was small blessing that the Inka'ata's legend was created after his soul had ridden the great white steed to join the ancestors in the unseen world.

'You will depart from us a boy and come back a man. Now go. Your fate rests in Ulekanan,' intoned Wole.

One by one, they turned their backs on him. Mbala stared at their backs. He had a question. With a sigh, he spun about and headed towards Ulekanan, the City of Echoes, or that was the nearest translation from The Arcane. No, there was no point to his questions. Only those to be enstooled Inka'ata ever set foot into the ancient ruin, and Ulekanan was not to be spoken about. The sun on his naked bottom was a whip to his steps.

Mbala needed more time. More time to practise the spear against an opponent who was not trying to stick it in his gut. The more he thought of it, he accepted what he had always known; he had never wanted to be Inka'ata. Mbala wanted to stare at girls and steal kisses in the shadows. He wanted to listen to the stories of old man Semaj's stories of the hero who had to go mad in order to find the wisdom to save the world, or the one who was so lucky that his losses were wins in truth. Now Mbala could do with that kind of luck.

I Robin Irie

Ankle deep in the loose sand, Mbala looked up at the great walls of Ulekanan and marvelled. The mud walls rose a hundred spans tall and seemed untouched by the harshness of the desert weather. The legend of Ulekanan said that it had been standing longer than memory. The only truth known about it was that it killed those not having the blood of kings. That thought made Mbala shiver. He had seen the doubt in his father's eyes. What if he wasn't worthy? He looked over his shoulder and saw the tents going up. He could turn around and go back, but that would mean abdication, and the only way to abdicate was to drink of the stop-heart root.

Steeling himself, Mbala stepped through the arched gateway. It took three strides to clear the thickness of the wall, and he stood gaping. A carpet of grass, no taller than half a finger's length in any place he could see, covered a courtyard at least fifty paces wide. The only blemish, and it could not be called that, was flowering shrubs that scattered bursts of colour amongst the green, above which clouds of butterflies fluttered, and trees, half again as tall as a man and laden with fruits of every kind.

How? Mbala looked around for attendants. Impossible! His feet were moving. He needed to feel the grass between his toes and smell the flowers. Contentment settled him. Who would make a place like this for no purpose but to be looked at? His hand crept up to pluck a fruit.

Chatter came to him, breaking through his trancelike state. Mbala turned to see five people hurrying towards him. 'He comes, he comes,' they declaimed in one voice, jostling each other to get to the front. 'Oh, he comes.'

He took them in. Like carvings of the finest ebony made with the same hand, their beauty was striking. He could not tell one hairless head from the other, and he also could not tell man or woman apart, or whether the distinction existed.

They came to a halt before him.

'Choose me. Choose me,' they said one after the other.

Mbala swallowed and found his voice. 'Who are you?'

They looked at him, then at each other, 'Why do they always ask that?' they repeated after each other. Mbala found it jarring.

'We are the Echoes.'
'Echoes.'
'Echoes.'
'Echoes of you.'
'Echoes into you.'
'Echoes of all.'

Mbala raised his hands to his head; it was too much. 'Choose me. Choose me,' they started up again.

He pointed at random. 'Why should I choose you?'

The Echo – that was a crazy name – stepped forward and held up a lukasa, a memory board not unlike those used by the Men of Memory. 'I can give you the knowledge of women.'

Mbala squinted at the artefact. 'Why?'

'Why?' the Echo repeated. 'Because it's what you've always wanted. You do like dreaming about women and wishing you were stronger, more handsome...'

Mbala had heard enough. 'How will that help me to be a good Inka'ata?' It was the truth, but he was a man now, not some moon-eyed boy.

'It will make you happy. That is what you want.'

Mbala's finger moved to the next in line. 'And you?'

'I will show you the way of the brave. Leave behind the coward and I will make you brave and give you the courage to match your heroes. It is what you want.'

I Robin Irie

It was what Mbala wanted. In his mind's eye, he saw himself at the head of the horde, spear held high to strike the final blow to the Nabingis. A crushing end to this war. He opened his mouth to accept and thought of his father. What good would bravery do with a weak arm? Better to hear what the others had to offer.

'I will show you the way to be strong. No longer will you be held back by your crippled arm. Take your place beside your father in the stories,' said the third Echo. 'You know it's what you want.'

It was what he wanted. Mbala made his mind up. He looked at the last two. They seemed a little less eager than the rest. 'And you, 'he asked

'We give answers,' they said in unison.

'I am the Echo of the past,' said one, raising its memory board. 'A man who does not know where he is coming from does not know where he is going. He does not know who he is.'

The other raised its lukasa. 'A man who knows where he is going can avoid the pitfalls in his path.'

Mbala looked from identical face to identical face, all of them returning inviting looks. All his life, he had wanted to be the strong courageous warrior that women swooned after and men told stories about. He wanted it all, but he could only choose one. *Above all, the Inka'ata must be wise.* Wole's words pierced his thought.

Mbala raised his hand and pointed. 'I want to know who I am.'

The Echo of the past stepped closer and thrust its memory board towards Mbala. 'Choose your path'

'My path?' asked Mbala, staring at the symbols. They were alien to the ones he had spent a lifetime learning.

'Your path. Choose one and see with the eyes of your ancestors.'

The Echo Though the Ages

Mbala searched the lukasa. He focused on the symbol of an eye; it seemed right. He reached out and touched it. There was a flash of white light and his mind was consumed.

Sunlight thrust spears of light through the bamboo wattles, capturing motes of dust that mingled with the pungent smoke. Mbala saw ten men lounging in a circle, propped up on elbows, bamboo smoking tubes hanging from the corners of their mouths.

'It's gone too far, Nkanko,' said a man who seemed to be the youngest of the group. He scrunched up his face as if blocking some awful stench. 'Azari is a clan chief, and he's giving over his daughter to be married to them.' He fixed his gaze on the eldest who puffed idly on his smoking tube as he studied the mats on the floor.

'You have nothing to say?'

Nkanko raised his head and the two locked eyes. 'The way I heard it, Bayaro, the girl had her mind set on marrying the Nabingi boy.'

Bayaro's big hand clenched into a fist. 'Should that matter? It's not our way.'

'It's true, Nkanko,' said a third man. 'Every day more of our young people adopt Nabingi ways.'

'So you've often told me,' said Nkanko. He took a long pull on his smoking tube. 'What you have not yet told me is why that is a bad thing.'

Bayaro sat upright and threw his hand into the air. 'You see what I told you? His mind is enfeebled, or he's gone soft. He would have our bloodline diminished! He'll sit by as the Knen disappear.'

'If our blood mixes with theirs, how will we disappear? Will our blood not live on through future generations? You are young, Bayaro, but not too young to remember that it was our own people who attacked us and chased us out. The Nabingis took us in and gave us a home and this is how you act.'

Bayaro spat to the side then met the eyes of each man in the circle. One after the other, they nodded at him. 'What is the matter with you, old man? Is there none of the warrior left inside you? Would you have the lion kiss the feet of the gazelle and tell it thanks for dinner. The Knen will never be like these weaklings, not while I draw breath.'

Nkanko read the faces and his shoulders slumped. 'I know more of the warrior than I wish I did, Bayaro. Knen clan fighting Knen clan for simple insults. While we butchered each other over grazing rights, the Nabingis built cities. How is a man skilled at taking a life greater than he who makes three measures of millet grow where only one used to grow?'

Nine faces stared back at Nkanko while silence held.

'It is as I told you', said Bayaro. 'Nkanko is no longer fit to lead us. I say that we need a new chief.' He looked around the circle again, then removed a knife from his belt and laid it in front of him. 'Who stands with me?'

A look of resignation settled on Nkanko's face as each man laid down his blade.

'It is unanimous, Nkanko,' said Bayaro. He looked at the old man like a cat who had stumbled upon a chick that had fallen from its nest. 'Will you drink of the root or will you dishonour us by having us spill your blood?'

The scene flickered and changed.

A stillness, amplified by the heat and humidity, settled on the land. Great carrion birds took to wing, their murderous quarrel making plain their displeasure at being disturbed from their bountiful feast. They flapped around, spreading the stench of blood, gore and rot.

Bayaro strutted on, his axe brown with old, dried blood strapped to his back and his long-bladed spear hanging loose in his grip. If he was troubled by the bodies that littered the field, he showed no sign. The one thousand Knen warriors that followed in his wake copied him – some of them. More than a few men had their hands covering nose and mouth, while others tried to look anywhere but at bloated corpses, some of which had eyes plucked out and lips eaten away to give the effect of rictus smiles. Not to be out done by the vultures, black flies swarmed in their millions as their white offspring wriggled and writhed in some unholy dance.

One of those closest to Bayaro stopped and bent double. Vomit shot from his mouth as his body shook from the effect. As if taking that to be permission, scores of men started emptying their stomachs, some of them falling to their knees. The column halted as men stopped to pat a companion's back or rest a sympathetic hand on a shoulder.

Bayaro stopped and surveyed his men, his disgust written plain on his face. 'Get up, you sons of dogs!' his voice rang out, causing more vultures to take to the air. 'I said get up!'

Men struggled to their feet, some with a little help.

'You are Knen and you will not show weakness. The next man who does will be tied to the whipping post.'

He resumed his walk to the royal compound. The men scrambled after him.

'Come on, pick your feet up!' he shouted over his shoulder. 'They are preparing a feast in the palace.'

Whether it was the promise of food and liquor, or the urge to flee the display of death, they quickened their steps.

Not all men revelled in the feast inside the captured Nabingi palace. Some drank heavily of strong liquor and picked at their vegetables, leaving chunks of meat untouched on their platters. Bayaro was not counted among these. He tore into a slice of roasted goat, ignoring the grease that leaked between his fingers and down his hand. Licking his lips, he inspected the spoils of conquest: young women all, and of noble birth. Bayaro squatted before one and used his free hand to lift her face to meet his. Her glare should have singed his hair.

'Princess Anache,' he said, the corners of his mouth curling into a smile. 'It pleases me to tell you that your station has improved. You are to be made my wife and my Shiata.'

The princess's expression did not change, but her full lips parted, and a glob of spittle flew into Bayaro's face. He released her chin and wiped at his face, breaking out in a wide grin. Without warning, his hand swung, backhanding her across the face. The princess was thrown back by the blow and lay still. She bled from the nose, red streams on black skin.

The merriment paused.

Getting to his feet, Bayaro looked around. 'What is the matter?' he asked of the musicians. 'Keep playing. Play something triumphant.'

The music picked back up and Bayaro grabbed a mug of liquor and went to join a man standing at a window, looking toward the field of death.

'You do not seem to be celebrating our triumph, Ade,' said Bayaro.

Ade, a head shorter than Bayaro, passed his hand over a head liberally scattered with white amongst tight coils. 'There aren't enough vultures,' he said.

'What?' ask Bayaro, taking a mouthful from his mug.

'There aren't enough vultures. We will have to organise burial parties unless we plan to abandon the whole district and let nature take its course.'

Bayaro grimaced. 'The men won't like it.'

'Even so,' said Ade.

They stood in silence for a while. It was Bayaro who broke it. 'Cowards. Imagine leaving your war dead like that.'

Ade raised his head to meet Bayaro's face. 'They chose to live.'

'Too many of them got away. A soon as we are settled, we will hunt them in their mountain hideouts.'

'Don't you think we have done enough, Bayaro? Don't you think we have done too much?'

Bayaro squinted at Ade, confusion on his face. 'What are you talking about?'

'The ordinary people want to live their lives in peace without caring too much who rules over them. They want their crops to grow and their family to be happy. Now we have every Nabingi fleeing for the mountain. We are herdsmen, Bayaro. What do we know about building cities or maintaining dams? It seems that we have managed to chase off or kill the people we need, and in so doing, we have taught them the way of the warrior. This war will go on for a long time.'

Bayaro laughed and shook his head. 'Ade, my friend, you always worry too much.'

Flicker.

It was a grand room. The floor was covered in thick red, green and gold carpets. In one corner, painted men chanted and blew smoke from earthenware bowls. With his head propped up by a cushion, Bayaro was much older. He did not suffer from decrepitude; he was more like weathered stone. His jaw was clenched, and he groaned fitfully.

Sitting beside his sleeping pallet, Anache looked on with hard eyes as the healer peeled away the bandage on Bayaro's stomach. The Inka'ata yelped and cursed as the cloth came loose, stiff with congealed blood and pus. The healer reached for a mug and brought it to the Bayaro's lips, but he gave his head a vigorous shake.

'Here, give it to me,' said Anache, taking the mug from the healer. She brought it to her husband's lips. 'Come, husband. It will help the pain and there is no shame in this.'

Bayaro allowed himself to be fed the thick liquid. In moments, he was still except for his eyes that searched the Shiata's face. Bodily odours permeated the room as the royal bowels relaxed.

'Tell me truthfully, healer, how bad is it?' asked the Shiata.

The healer did not look at her. 'I will not lie to you, nana. The odds are exceedingly short on gut wounds. All I can do is keep it clean as his fate is now in the hands of the Great Spirits.'

The Shiata nodded and adopted a thoughtful look. She watched in silence as the healer cleansed the wound and replaced the poultice.

'He had always wanted to die in battle, you know?' said the Shiata, speaking into the silence. 'Blazing like a comet that lights up the heavens, leaving a memory imprinted on the world.'

'Death comes when it will, nana,' said the healer. 'And the memory that lives on is the one that we pass on through the ages.'

The Shiata nodded.

'The wound was taken in battle. How the end came is something the men of memory can be generous with,' continued the healer.

Long after the healer and painted priests had left, the Shiata held a quiet vigil beside the Inka'ata's bed. A moan from him drew her attention and she reached out and held his hand. He returned a feeble squeeze.

For a while longer, she sat like that.

'I stopped hating you a long time ago,' said the Shiata. 'Not because you deserve it, but for my own sake and for the sake of the children I have borne you. Children who are half Knen and half Nabingi, but whom you have raised to hate the Nabingi half of themselves.'

Another lengthy silence intervened before she spoke again. 'I too may have been complicit because I have sat by and watched the lies become truths. I have not told them that the father they love and worship is a brute that usurped and butchered their mother's people. I could never bring myself to do that. You have always wanted to know the location of the city of the ancient, but I have kept it from you. I will tell it to my sons in the hope that there they will find wisdom to be better men.'

She leaned over and wiped the sweat beading on his forehead. 'Go on,' she said. 'Ride your white stallion to meet your ancestors. I forgive you. For my sake and the children's, I do.'

Bayaro's hand quivered and his lips moved, causing her to bring her ear to his mouth.

'Thank you,' he whispered. 'Thank you.'

And Bayaro the Great, first Inka'ata of the Knen, gave up the ghost.

Flicker

Mbala shook his head to clear his mind as the memories of the visions embedded themselves into his mind. He looked about to find himself outside the walls of Ulekanan. Solid wall stood where the gate was. Mbala breathed deeply. The Knen - his Knen - were the usurpers. The thought left him sullied. Maybe he should not be surprised. Hunters told the stories, so the lion was never the hero. He was supposed to be of pure Knen stock, but his whole existence was a lie.

Realising he held something, Mbala looked down to find a lukasa in his hand. It was blank except for a single symbol carved into it, the symbol for knowing. To know is to be wise. The words echoed through his mind as he passed a finger over them. Mbala set out for the tents, thoughts tumbling over each other. Knowing what he now knew, there was no hunger to lead the war against the Nabingis - not with the zeal that he would require. After all, they were his people too, people of his blood.

As his bare feet crunched on the sand, the seed of an idea began to form in his mind, the seed of hope. He lifted his head and looked towards the tents where they waited for him. Mbala the peacemaker? Maybe, but for that he would need the luck of the one-eyed gambler from the stories.

ECHOES PAST AND PRESENT
By

Jane Andrews

The sun beat down upon the diverse people who thronged the busy marketplace. At this time of year, the olfactory cacophony was overwhelming as the odour of livestock merged with unwashed bodies. Pip glanced at his master, busy arguing over the price of something and slipped away into the crowd, his eyes searching for Will. Tomorrow, they would be back in the nailer's yard, but for now, they needed to make the most of the Bull Ring market and everything that was on offer.

He quickly found the other lad. Will was watching a wrestling match, his eyes following the shirtless men as they grappled with each other in a space cleared for the purpose. Perspiration beaded the faces of the combatants, each as determined as the other to win the purse. The darker of the two was larger with well defined muscles that stood out like whipcord on his back and shoulders, but the redhead was agile and cunning and Pip thought him a more likely winner.

Will started when Pip nudged his arm.

'Come and have some ale,' Pip urged. They might find a pie seller too, he reflected, although he certainly didn't have the requisite penny and he was sure Will didn't either. Thirst was a more pressing matter than hunger in this weather; he was used to going without food in the middle of the day.

His friend looked reluctant to leave before the bout was over. Relenting for a moment, Pip did not press him further, waiting with Will until the redhead had triumphed

– if a broken nose and bruised side could be called a victory. They slipped away from the murmur of the other spectators and made their way towards one of the women hawking ale from a large vat atop a little wooden platform on wheels, thankful for the tall, pointed hat that marked her out as a brewer. She might have been hard to find otherwise in this sea of merchants and tradesmen.

As the warm liquid slid down his throat, Pip let his eyes travel over the terrain. It seemed the whole community was here – as you might well expect on market day. More people than he could count filled the narrow gaps between stalls; and then there were the peddlers too with their trays full of ribbons and trinkets, or the ones bearing pies. His mouth watered at the smell of them.

For a moment, something alien to the scene before him glistened in the sunlight. He blinked at the sight of the tall, black structure with its shiny sides like polished marble. He looked again and it was gone, but even that brief glimpse had unsettled him.

'Did you see anything strange just then?' he asked Will.

'What do you mean by 'strange'?' Will's tone was guarded.

'Just for a moment, I thought I saw...' He paused, not wanting Will to think it was the ale talking.

'...A black tower in the middle of the marketplace,' Will finished. 'I saw it too.'

'So where is it now?' Pip asked, looking once more at the spot where the strange thing had appeared and disappeared. In its place, the old, stone fountain sat where it always did, water bubbling from the stone fish's mouth in the centre.

Will looked troubled. 'There's something not right about this,' he said slowly. 'I don't know... It just feels wrong somehow.'

As if in a dream, they found their feet taking them towards the fountain, almost as if something unseen were calling to them. Everyone knew the water wasn't safe to drink, but today, Pip found himself longing for the sensation of the droplets on his skin. He reached his hand towards the cascading water and felt... Nothing. His hand remained dry as bone.

Out of the corner of his eye, he could see Will doing the same thing. Then, as their hands pressed further into the illusion of water, he felt the smooth, polished surface of the structure he'd seen earlier and his mind was suddenly jolted into a different version of Brummagem: a reality that seemed terrifying compared with what he already knew.

The noise deafened him. There seemed to be ten times as many people – or more – than there had been just moments ago. And the clothing... Some of the women had bare legs and wore their hair loose, unrestricted by a cap or bonnet. The livestock was gone and in its place loomed strange buildings that looked like nothing he had seen before, while in the distance, monstrous looking creatures rumbled past, stopping only to spew people out of their mouths. *Is this Hell?* he thought desperately.

'You see it too, don't you?' Will murmured.

Shaking, Pip withdrew his hand. 'This is a bad place,' he told Will, thankful to see normality return as he lost contact with the structure. 'We must leave.'

But his friend did not move: instead, he remained staring into the fountain, his expression rapt, his eyes bright with something akin to fanaticism.

'Thousands of stars,' he whispered. 'Thousands and thousands of stars.'

'Will...' Pip was beginning to feel frightened now. 'It's not real. It's witchcraft or some kind of sorcery, showing us things that aren't there. Terrible things.'

He grabbed Will's hand and yanked him away from the fountain. Will let out a roar of frustration, then tried to plunge his hand back into the water; but Pip planted his heels and held onto his friend, preventing him from reaching his goal.

'Let go of me, Pip.' Will's voice held a note of warning.

'It's not safe,' Pip panted, his hold beginning to weaken.

Suddenly, Will broke free and darted to the fountain. Thrusting his hand into the water, he began feeling for the invisible column, the turned to Pip, his face full of anguish. 'Why did you do that?' he cried. 'Whatever it was, it's gone.'

The mood was spoilt for the rest of the day. Will could not forgive Pip for 'rescuing' him from the mysterious object and the strange sensations it provoked; and Pip felt sure that his friend was under a spell and was rapidly losing his mind. As daylight gradually faded into dusk and wares were packed away, Pip saw Will cast a longing look in the direction of the fountain and knew that the strange object still had a hold on the other lad.

Trudging back to Moseley, Pip was aware of the silence forming an invisible wall between them. The air seemed heavy with unspoken recriminations, but it was not his fault, he told himself fiercely: Will was the one who had wanted to lose himself in the fountain's spell. Had his friend seen the same things he had? he wondered.

'I did the right thing,' he burst out suddenly. 'Those *things* – they were eating people and spitting them out! How could you want anything to do with that?'

Will stopped walking, fixing Pip with an expression of bewilderment. 'I don't know what you saw,' he said slowly, 'but the world the fountain showed me was beautiful. We were floating in the sky, surrounded by stars. I think we might have been in heaven.'

'That's blasphemy!' Pip said, shaking at even the thought of it. 'If Parson heard you now...'

Will's mouth set in an obstinate line. 'What does he know? He hasn't seen what I did. You neither.'

He refused to say anything more for the remainder of their journey.

Later that night, Pip was wakened by the sound of someone getting up from his place on the floor and quietly stealing through the yard. He thought he already knew who the culprit was, but his eyes searched in the gloom to make sure anyway. John and Harry were still fast asleep – John snoring lightly as he always did – but Will's space was empty. An uneasy feeling wrapped itself around Pip's throat, constricting his breathing. He knew where Will was heading, and the thought terrified him. As silently as he could, he got to his feet and padded after his friend.

He waited until they had left the yard behind before making Will aware of his presence. 'Come back,' he hissed. 'If Master finds out...'

'You don't understand.' Will kept on walking, making Pip run to catch up with him. 'Learning a trade, having a roof over my head – none of that matters anymore.'

'You're bewitched!' As Pip spoke the damning words, he regretted them instantly; but Will just nodded.

'Maybe I am. But I'd rather go back to that fountain and see what I saw all over again than spend the rest of my life making nails and other bits and pieces – even if they do burn me for it.'

Pip felt torn. He'd grown up with Will; had been overjoyed when Master Robert had chosen to take them both on as apprentices. He didn't want to lose his friend; but he had the same mistrust as anyone else these days for anything that couldn't be explained by common sense or the Bible.

'What if I don't tell anyone?' he offered. 'What if I come with you and wait while you see what you have to see, and then we both go back to Master Robert and carry on as before?'

This time, Will stopped walking. He turned to face Pip, his features wearing an expression Pip couldn't fathom.

'Very well, then. Come with me, and then see if you change your mind.'

'I'm not putting my hand in the fountain again,' Pip warned.

'You can please yourself.' Will took a deep breath. 'We need to hurry, though: the portal won't stay open forever.'

He set off again, leaving Pip to wonder what his friend had meant.

Hurrying along in the dim half-light cast by the pale moon, Pip struggled to keep up with Will. It was as if the other lad were propelled by some arcane force that dragged him back towards the marketplace and the mysterious fountain. He knew he should have stayed in the yard, but there was something that bound him to Will: he couldn't explain it; just knew that he had to be by his side. A moth fluttered past his face and the papery wings stirred some kind of distant echo within him, something too faint for him to grasp. For a brief moment, something flickered across his mind: an impression of flight and air; but once again, the memory eluded him, hovering just out of reach.

The night-time air was cooler than he'd first thought and he shivered involuntarily, wishing he'd had the foresight to bring his blanket with him. He could have wrapped it around his shoulders like a makeshift cloak. Stealing a glance at Will, still striding ahead and seemingly unaffected by the temperature, he found his thoughts dwelling on their friendship. They had always known each other, or at least, that was what it felt like. But now, try as he might, he could not form a recollection of anything from their childhood. It seemed as if their lives had not begun until they started working in the nailer's yard.

Will spoke, his voice echoing strangely in the near-dark. 'We're nearly there. Stay close to me and do what I tell you.'

Pip felt like retorting that Will wasn't his master; but instead, he bided his tongue and obeyed.

The marketplace was deserted at this time. Pip gazed at the thoroughfares which had been so busy only hours ago and felt a wave of longing for... what? Again, he tried to capture the memory; yet once more, it remained out of reach.

'It's getting stronger,' Will muttered under his breath. 'We don't even need to touch it now: just being near it's enough.'

The words meant no sense to Pip.

Then, suddenly, reality swirled and the nightmarish vision he had seen earlier came flooding back – except this time, he wasn't just a spectator to what was going on: he was living it. The cobbles under their feet gave way to a strange, flat substance – grey and dismal. Tall buildings like nothing he had ever seen before towered over them both, their fronts replaced with a clear substance that looked like glass – but who in their right mind would build something with a glass front? Garish colours danced all over signs painted upon the lintels; he recognised some of the letters but he could not form them into words he understood. And the people! Hordes of them streamed past, not even looking at him: all of them caught up in their own busy-ness. They did not look like the people he knew for their hair and skin was as various as their clothing: some wore next to nothing at all whilst others were covered from head to foot. Those who had companions talked loudly in accents he did not know; and many of those on their own held trinkets in their hands and seemed to be conversing with them. His heart beating in terror, he looked for Will, but the other lad was nowhere in sight.

Sinking to the ground, Pip crouched, head in hands, wishing the spectacle away. How could anyone want to live like that? he wondered. Then time and space shimmered again, and he found himself standing in a vast, empty chamber clutching Will's hand.

'Pip!' Will's voice sounded relieved. 'I thought for a moment I'd lost you.'

'Where are we?' Why did Will sound so confident when he, Pip, felt so uncertain?

Will took a deep breath. 'We're where we've always been – or at least, where we've been for the last six thousand years.'

None of it made any sense. How could Will claim that they were where they had always been? A moment ago, he had been in Brummagem's marketplace; and before that, he and Will had been on the road; and before that...

Stop trying to understand. Will's thought spoke directly into Pip's mind. *Clear your thoughts and let me show you.*

And so he watched as history unfolded, caught up in it all much as he had been in the nightmare of the mutated marketplace. At first, he saw nothing but darkness, and then a brilliant burst of light shattered the inky blackness and pinpointed the heavens with countless stars. He focused his attention on one that seemed to glow less brightly than the others and found himself tumbling towards it, drawn by some unknown force. From his vantage point in the firmament above the terrain, he watched barren ground crack open and springs issue forth, gradually swelling to become rivers and oceans. Vegetation sprang up where the earth was watered: plants and trees bloomed into existence; woods and forests began to dot the planet. Next, life began to teem in the water: he was aware of arthropods, then crustaceans and fish moving beneath the waves. After a while, creatures crawled out of sea onto dry land, limbs forming as they did so. Some of the lizards scuttled into the forest; others stretched out on rocks; and another group flexed their powerful forelegs into wings and flew into the sky. Gradually, the forest lizards evolved into sub-species, differing in size and shape. Some hunted the smaller ones, whilst others were content to munch grass and leaves, but as the temperature cooled, one by one, the creatures faded into dust.

Pip felt a lump in his throat as he watched, but Will squeezed his hand. *That was but the beginning. Now Act Two begins.*

And life continued. The new creatures had long, shaggy hair on their bodies and the winged ones had feathers. Some of the groups contained vaguely humanoid beings; time rolled by and he watched the stooping apes straighten into men.

Centuries of progress flashed by in no time at all; then, as Pip began to recognise places and faces, the timeline slowed and he and Will were standing in the marketplace that afternoon, with both of them about to put their hands in the fountain.

'How are you doing this?' Pip sounded fearful. 'How did you make everything disappear and then come back again? Is it witchcraft?'

He felt rather than heard Will's reply. *Pip, my child, what you are experiencing now in Brummagem's town centre is only an echo of what once was.*

'No!' Pip cried wildly. 'What you say isn't true? How can this be an echo? Why, 'tis the Year of our Lord, 1362 – you know that as well as I do!'

Clear your thoughts, Will repeated.

And then they were back in the nightmare vision he'd had, and it was just as garish and as noisy and as frightening as it had been on the other two occasions that day. But this time, he was aware of Will at his side, holding his hand tightly; and his panic dissipated and his fear faded away.

What you are experiencing, said Will's voice in his mind, *is Brummagem – or Birmingham as it is now known – in the Year of our Lord, 2020. Mankind has made great strides in industry and technology, and any one of these people you see around you carries in his or her pocket enough artificial intelligence to send him or her to the stars. Oh, Man is proud of his achievements: he does not need to toil like his ancestors for machines do most of his work for him; neither does he need to worry about becoming sick or even dying, for modern medicine is rapidly becoming effective enough to treat any and every ailment, and he can even choose to have his dying body frozen – to be revived at a later date when scientists will have perfected their serum for eternal life. He has climbed the tallest mountains; he has plumbed the depths of the deepest sea; he has even travelled across the galaxy, in search of other planets to populate and destroy – for once he has used all of Mother Earth's resources, she will no longer be of use to him.*

Pip's eyes were wide with horror. 'Is this an echo of the future?' he asked uncertainly. 'Or is it now?'

It is neither, Will replied. *What you have just seen is but another echo of the dim and distant past. It was necessary for you to see the potential harm of the twenty-first century that you might be better equipped to understand what comes next.*

A series of images danced across Pip's brain. Crowds of people thronged streets, then toppled like dominoes as bullets hailed into them. Bombs exploded in the midst of innocent people, flames flowering into the sky as women and children were torn apart by the blast. Limbs littered the ground; bodies burned alive. The earth cried out as it was scorched by Man's selfishness. Forests were razed to the ground; the oceans' waters became brown and lifeless. Huge carcasses rotted on beaches, whilst further inland, entire species were hunted to extinction so that rich narcissists could impress their friends. The stench of death was everywhere, and Pip wept.

Do you now recall what happened? Will's voice was gentle.

A sunbeam of clarity pierced the fog in Pip's mind and, as his confusion cleared, he saw past, present and future existing at the same time, echo layered upon echo, never ending, never beginning. 'We were the Chosen ones,' he said, beginning to remember.

The world is collapsing in on itself. Shouts and screams fill the air as mushroom clouds rise into the atmosphere. Pip feels torn, wanting to stay with his family but knowing that he has been selected to live. Beside him, his father, Will, squeezes his hand. 'I wish we could take them with us,' he says, 'but the algorithm didn't deem them suitable.'

How can he walk away from his mother and sisters, from girls who are just six and eleven, from the woman who gave birth to him and has nurtured him for all of his fifteen years?

His father hardens his voice. 'You can die with them, or you can save the human race.'

And Pip wipes the tears from his eyes and walks aboard the shuttle that will carry him and his father and the other ten Chosen Ones to the waiting starship that will be their home for the next thousand years or more.

'You're my father,' he accused.

Will's face shifted to take on the features that Pip remembered.

'There were twelve of us altogether – we were supposed to escape the Earth's destruction and start the human race all over again – a bit like a modern-day Noah's Ark.'

Will nodded. *We sailed through stars for millennia, searching for a new Earth – a planet where we could do things better. Everything that mankind had achieved was with us: all the music, all the art, all the literature; all the scientific breakthroughs and new medicines and most useful technologies. We had everything we needed to recreate human society with only the best parts of what we had known before; but time and time again, within but a few generations, each new Earth began to go the way of the original. In time, we realised that the only way for man to live in relative peace was without the technology he had come to rely on.*

So we decided to recreate an earlier timeline, Pip finished, continuing the conversation telepathically without being aware of it. *We chose a time with no visible technology, but we combined the people's simple lifestyle with hidden benefits for their health and well-being.*

How could he have forgotten all of this? He was the one who had suggested adding anti-virus medication to the ale so that people had a better chance of surviving colds and flu and the plague.

We don't usually live amongst the people, do we? he asked next.

No, his father agreed, *we usually keep our distance. We have little in common with the creatures we have grown on our ship and even less with their children and their children's children. We have had thousands of years to evolve into the higher life forms we are today – which is why we are now often mistaken for angels. It seems that religion and superstition will never die, no matter how far we venture into the galaxy or how many millennia have passed since the days of the original Earth. We cloned our own DNA and grew specimens that we thought would be without human failings; but still there seems to be an inbuilt longing to worship a higher power and to believe that Someone is in charge of everything.*

So, why did it all change? Pip wanted to know. This was a part of the recent past that he could not remember. *Why have we been living the lives of the unevolved when we know what it is to walk amongst the stars?*

Will sighed. *We created an artificial world – one which could easily be controlled from our echo chamber here. The planet itself is real, but we populated it with the memories of a long ago era – a time the ancients called 'The Middle Ages'. You and I volunteered to live among our creation: we believed we could model the pattern of behaviour that would help humankind to survive.* He looked at his son and Pip was aware of the intense fatherly pride that emanated from him. *We chose to relinquish our memories and store the echoes until they would be needed once more.*

The obelisk, Pip said, remembering. *When we caught sight of it earlier today, we were looking at the portal that would bring us back here. That was our escape hatch.*

And the fountain was an illusion to hide the structure, Will finished. *But when you inadvertently touched it, echoes of the past began to seep through and you saw a version of Brummagem akin to the one we had escaped. Your medieval mindset could not understand – and so you responded in fear.*

And what about you? Why weren't you afraid like I was?

I touched the side of the portal for longer than you did, Will admitted, *and in that moment, I knew everything. Our work here is done: we are free to leave the humans to fumble through life on their own. This time, we think they have a chance to get things right.*

'When you say, 'leave the humans',' Pip found he was speaking out loud once more, 'do you mean abandon them completely?'

We will still observe them from a distance – but we will not intervene.

Pip let the implications sink in. Will – his father – was telling him that the life they had both lived here so far was a lie; and now he had the chance to leave that deception behind and to be himself again. Still, he faltered.

'And what about the lives we've made for ourselves in this play-world?' he asked now. 'What about our families, and Master Robert, and John and Harry, and the Parson, and...'

When they wake in the morning, we will be but a distant echo, Will told him. *Our own memories have expanded to hold the whole of history: we are walking echo chambers; but their minds are still small and unformed and they will forget us quickly.* He placed a reassuring hand on Pip's shoulder. *The family you spoke of is not your family. Your real mother and sisters are here with us.*

For a moment, his face flickered and Pip saw his mother standing there in Will's place. The image shimmered into his older sister, then into the younger one.

We can be anything – and anyone – we want to be, Will said. *We are not bound like those pitiful humans to one body, one existence.*

Pip thought of the memories he had: of the woman he knew as 'Mother' in the ancient timeline; of the exhilaration of chopping wood in the winter and the gaiety of watching the dancing around the village maypole. Despite knowing that these things were mere illusions, he was loath to leave them. Once, he had sacrificed his godhood to become like these lowly humans; he could not abandon them now: they were embedded in his soul.

'Why did you choose to appear as the age that I am rather than being my father?' he demanded. In this most recent lifetime, he, Pip, had been the age of the boy who had set off on a shuttle to save the world, but his father had disguised himself in a completely different persona.

Will gazed into his son's eyes.

'When we lived on the real earth,' he said slowly, 'I was always too busy to pay you much attention. I was proud of you for doing well in school and for working hard, but it was your mother who really knew you. From the time you were born, she talked to you, sang to you, poured her humanity into you. She is the reason for your compassion – and why you were the twelfth person to be chosen to save the species. The rest of us would have given up the first time the humans failed on their new earth; but you always believed in them – always had hope for the future.

You volunteered to live in this new society when we set up the colony here; and I agreed to accompany you, thinking that it would enable us to bond. I wanted to give you all the friendship and attention I withheld from you when you were growing up in the twenty-first, and so I made myself into the sort of person I thought could support you and help you and chose a set of false memories for myself that would help me to live as Will, a nailer's apprentice, alongside my own son.'

He spoke the words out loud, but Pip knew his father was still in his head and aware of everything his son planned to do.

'You know why I have to stay,' he said softly.

Will nodded.

'I'll miss you,' Pip continued, his voice trembling a little. 'I've had my father at my side for thousands of years – it will be strange knowing you're not there anymore.'

'You won't be aware of it,' Will said quickly. 'You'll return to exactly where you were before the portal called us away. When you wake up in the nailer's yard, you might have a vague awareness of there being something missing – but it won't seem important. Within a day or two, you'll have forgotten I ever existed.'

Putting his arms around Pip, he hugged him fiercely. Surprised, Pip hugged back.

'So much of your essential essence is already in this chamber that it will be almost like having you here with me.' Will was putting on a brave face, but Pip felt his father's sadness.

'I won't see you again, will I?' It was more a statement than a question.

'You won't see me or even remember me, but I'll be watching you for as long as...' Will's voice trailed off. 'For as long as you live your human life,' he finished.

When Pip was gone, his echo would remain: it was etched upon his father's heart.

THE COLOSSAL MIMIC OCTOPUS
By

Chris Murtagh

The camouflage of the colossal mimic octopus has one drawback. There are few things in the sea vast enough for the octopus to mimic, and the intellect of the colossal mimic octopus is such that it is one of the few animals capable of boredom.

A flourish of tentacles, like a magician rolling cards over their fingers, and three humpback whales are swimming in unison. A hypnotic swirl of pigments across its chromatophores and an innocent coral reef is conjured into being. A quick puff out of its head body and a nuclear submarine toddles through the deep.

A wonderful trick, but there are only so many sunken Spanish Galleons a cephalopod can make.

It goes something like this: an innocent shark or squid, whale or dolphin sees what might be a friendly bunch of lost relatives or a tasty shoal of tuna, so it swims on in to investigate until it slams into an invisible eyelid, which flips open. An eye as big as a Ford Fiesta is everything. It gives away no hint of intelligence or emotion, only cold elegance, as all becomes beak and suckers and enveloping limbs.

Usually, when a vehicle of yellow metal and domed glass purrs close, the octopus knows the drill. Get still, fade to black, wait for it to dawdle by. Nothing to eat here. This is the reason why the colossal mimic octopus is not known to science.

Beside the submersible pilot sits an entrepreneur. He has made his money selling t-shirts and records, and then plane tickets and carbonated drinks, credit cards and vodka, lipstick, underwear, loans, finally just his name, his image, his appearance linked to any other thing he can conjure up.

He has long shaggy hair. Wooden bangles on his arms. A flowing casual checked shirt. A well-worn t-shirt with a grey alien head printed on it. His carefree eccentricity is further stamped by the 'Welcome to Birmingham' postcard that is pinned to the front of the computer monitor, a keepsake from a store he used to own.

The spotlight of the vehicle finds a rectangle of yellow metal. Another sub down here? It bobs and hovers just at the edge of sight.

'Let's go say hello,' says the businessman, never one to miss a networking opportunity.

It leads them deeper into the abyss.

'It must have spotted us . . . Why no lights?'

A pressure gauge starts to blip red.

'What is that?'

Some kind of thin antenna array passes beside them, filled with round dishes. Could it have fallen from a ship? From an oil rig telecoms tower?

'Buildings?'

Thick brutalist facades slide by.

'Am I on something?'

'If we are, it's good stuff,' says the pilot.

They chase it through heavy silhouettes.

A tiny cathedral.

Long rows of metal market stalls.

On the ocean floor, they find a boxy shopping centre leading down to a bulbous hubcap-clad, curving blue form with a stubby tower just off in the distance.

'Who could build all this down here?'

The other sub has stopped a few metres in front of them. It's not a sub, only sub-like. Its robotic arms look more like tentacles. And the glass doesn't shine.

The Colossal Mimic Octopus

They set down directly opposite and watch as the object in front of them stops being a sub-like thing, becomes a cascade of wooden beads trickling away in a checked pattern, kicking up sand from the ocean floor.

It is revealed.

'Mind control! I knew it.'

A white grey being, the finest puppet the octopus has ever created, a manipulation of tentacle, floats towards them.

'They're real! They're real!'

The alien reaches out with a thin hand, its large head billowing just behind it.

The humans press their hands to the glass of the submersible, their hearts pounding.

For a few glorious moments, they share a communication deeper than words, and then the alien is consumed in a splurt of black ink and a kick of sand. Everything becomes normal ocean bed.

The two men blink at the darkness all around them, grasping each other's arms.

'It was the most incredible adventure of my life,' the businessman will tell the cameras later. 'I was touched by an alien. I could sense a supreme intelligence. It was magical.' And he is more right than he will ever know.

THE CROSSING PLACE
by

Hazel Ward

The broken chain rattled against the door as it closed. I dropped my keys on the hall table, then noticed where they'd landed. Next to hers. They hadn't taken them, then? I held hers. Inhaled their scent. They smelt of metal. They were keys. What was I expecting? Shit. This was going to be harder than I thought.

They'd done a good job of clearing up. Nothing left to suggest the apartment had ever been a crime scene. Aside from the chain, everything looked normal. Except it wasn't. How could it be? She wasn't there.

Technically, I could have returned earlier but I left it as long as I could. Until the hotel bills were crippling me. But I was back at work now. I only needed to be here to sleep. I could go elsewhere for everything else.

I put my bag of essentials on the kitchen counter. Fresh milk, coffee, two bottles of Jack Daniels. All I needed. The fridge was rank. I binned the rotting food; turned on the tap and emptied the milk carton. Lumps of mould fell into the sink, broke up and slid down the hole. Just a half-finished bottle of wine left. We'd opened it on our last night together. She'd wanted to cane it but I had a two-day course and an early train the next day. I took a tentative swig. Not as good as that night but drinkable. I filled a glass and finished it off.

I threw in a chaser of JD. Dark sediment from the wine dregs swirled around the amber liquid. Time was, that would have been heresy, but I was less fussy than I used to be. I sat on the couch and gazed out of the full-length windows that curved around the room. She used to do that. I'd wake up some nights and find her there, staring into space. Lights shimmered, like stars, across the evening cityscape. It was beautiful. I hated it. It made me think of her. I took her keys and left.

Generally, I'm not a man of habit. But there I was, on my way to the Chinese Quarter, again. Hurst Street was buzzing. It was Tuesday. Not exactly a party night but it was that kind of area. I slipped through the crowds outside the Hippodrome, down a side street, towards the welcoming red glow of Kimmie's Kitchen. Kimmie was big on red. The place was like a scarlet palace. It was busy but they kept a table for me. I pulled up a red leatherette chair.

The waitress came straight over. 'Usual?' She didn't bother with the menu.

'Yeah.'

'I'll tell Kimmie you're here.'

Kimmie brought two whiskies. She wore a mandarin collared dress. Black satin, embroidered in red. Her working outfit. In her downtime she was strictly designer. She rested her chin on manicured fingers, 'Any news on Salina?'

'You ask me that every day, and every day I tell you, there's nothing.'

'So, stop coming here every day. Then I won't ask.'

She knew why I came here. Good as it was, it wasn't the food. I met Salina here. That simple. The first time I saw her I was sitting at this table. She was talking to Kimmie at the bar. They were old friends. There was something about her. The way she sat. The way she took me in. No hint of embarrassment. I had to stop myself staring. She brought me a drink over. It was beer in those days. She stayed. I don't believe in love at first sight, but, that night, something fell into place. Three months later, we moved in together.

I necked the whisky.

Kimmie signalled the barman for another, 'She wouldn't like to see you drinking like this.'

'So, stop giving it to me.'

She rolled her eyes, 'Your food's ready. Look after yourself, Ash.'

She left me to my Sichuan crispy beef and noodles. One of the few benefits of my new life. Salina couldn't give me a hard time about eating meat.

When I left, Kimmie told me not to come back tomorrow. She knew I would. It was raining. A steady drizzle. The kind that took a while to absorb. I pulled up my collar and stumbled home to sleep on the couch.

The urge to spew woke me early next morning. I'm not a big drinker but, since Salina went, I'd begun to appreciate the medicinal qualities of hard alcohol. Two shots were usually enough to blunt the edges. Yesterday, I'd let it get out of hand. I put it down to first night nerves.

I made myself respectable and went to work. It was still raining. When I got in, the DCI called me over to say they were scaling down on Salina's case. 'I'm sorry Ash, but we're at that point. You know how it is.'

What could I say? If it were me, I'd have done the same. Where do you go with a disappearance like Salina's? You start with those closest to her. Me. I last saw her that morning. She was still in bed when I kissed her goodbye. I last spoke to her in the evening when I called from the hotel. I tried her a few times the following day, but she didn't pick up. Once they ruled me out, there was nowhere else to look. When someone vanishes from an eighteenth-floor apartment that's locked from the inside, your options are limited.

The chief patted my shoulder, 'I knew you'd understand. There are some cases on your desk that need reviewing. Usual thing. Mark them up for either closure or Cold Cases.'

More cleaning up. I'd been back a month and that was all I'd been doing. They were easing me in, and it was killing me. The lack of Salina had opened up a void inside of me that couldn't be filled with housekeeping.

'When are you going to let me back into the real world?'

She gave me her reassuring smile. The one she reserved for the families of victims. 'Soon. You're doing well. Let's not rush things.'

My mood nosedived further when I saw the collection of old folders in my in-tray. The coffee and Danish behind them, lifted it slightly. Someone was leaving them every morning, since I came back. I looked around for signs of my anonymous benefactor. As usual, no one owned up. As usual, I shouted, 'Thank you.' The slightest smile flickered across a dozen faces.

The top of the pile provided little hope for distraction. Too much like those I'd been working on. Housework. I tried the bottom. A missing family man; last seen in Digbeth. I scanned the rest. Five missing persons in all. They had to be a mistake. The boss would never have sanctioned them. I could have told her. I could have stuck to housework. I kept my mouth shut and dug in.

The first few were typical runaways. I don't mean to belittle the loss of a loved one, especially now, but there's a pattern. They usually pack. Clothes, money, cards, passport. All, or a combination, of those things. Occasionally, they'll use a card after leaving. The hardest are those that take nothing. The potential homicides. Or suicides. But bodies turn up with suicides. You can't kill yourself, then hide your own body. Even if they've drowned themselves, they eventually float to the top.

The runaways went back in the tray. Two left. One was 2001. A missing drug dealer. The other, 2012. A twenty-one-year-old British Chinese woman, Lian Chen. No obvious reason to leave, except she'd been down after her best friend moved to Hong Kong. In her final year at Birmingham University, she had a research offer in the US. Her parents' statements suggested she was happy, sociable, and popular. Her friends confirmed her popularity but just before her disappearance she'd been anti-social and secretive.

The last person to see her was Amy Lin. They'd had lunch together. Amy wanted to go shopping, but Lian was meeting someone. They walked into town and parted company halfway along New Street. I couldn't put my finger on why, but Amy's statement didn't feel right. Her number was in the records. People don't generally change phone numbers if they can help it. Phones, yes. But we get attached to numbers. I tried it. It went to answerphone, 'Hi, this is Amy Lin. Leave a message.' Result.

'Miss Lin, this is Detective Inspector Ash Carter. I'm calling about the disappearance of Lian Chen. Could you call me back?' I left my number and hung up.

She rang within minutes. The first thing she said was, 'Have you found her?'

I explained I was reviewing the case and asked if we could meet. She worked a short walk away, at the BMAG. She'd be free in an hour.

'You know the Round Room? Wait for me under the statue of Lucifer.' Before I had a chance to argue, she hung up.

An hour later, I waited in the spot I'd met Salina on our second date. Her choice. She loved it. For a mathematician, she had a surprising fondness for art and history. We didn't talk much about her work. Truth be told, I avoided it. It went over my head. My ignorance embarrassed me. Salina was smart but she played it down. She was kind like that.

Amy Lin was slim but curvaceous with dark wavy curls that bounced in time with her steps. She sashayed across the room, like an old-style femme fatale. 'Inspector Carter?' She was taller than she looked. Nearly my height. From a distance, I'd guessed at full European. Close up, I reassessed. At least a quarter Chinese. She eyed my damp clothes. 'Still raining out there?'

We found a table in the museum café and I tried not to think about being there with Salina. 'I know it's been seven years, but can you talk me through the last time you saw Lian?'

'We had lunch in MinMin. We'd planned to go shopping, but ended up drinking in the Green Room.'

'You said in your statement, Lian was meeting someone?'

'Yes, but that was later. Before you inquire, she didn't say who. They asked me that before. I wish I'd asked her. Originally, we were going to go shopping, then split up, but we were talking so much. I remember being happy that she seemed her old self again. I didn't want to stop her, so I suggested a drink.'

'What did you talk about?'

She pouted. 'Gossip. University. Boys. Well, I talked about boys. Boys weren't Lian's scene.'

'She was gay?'

'She never said, but I think so. At least, I think she was in love with Mei. After Mei went, just hearing her name upset Lian. But she talked a lot about Mei that afternoon. In a happy way.'

'Mei? The friend who moved abroad?'

Another pout. 'Mei Li vanished without a trace. If she'd really gone to Hong Kong, she'd have written or called. She and Lian were really tight.'

Strange. The case notes said Lian's friend just left. If she really did vanish, why leave that out? Something else puzzled me, 'Which route did you take when you left the Green Room?'

The pout again – presumably, her thinking face. 'Up Hurst Street and Smallbrook Queensway. Along the side of the Rotunda. We said goodbye by the bull.'

'The bull? You're sure it wasn't further up New Street?'

'I was going to Selfridges. Why would I walk past it and then turn back?'

I knew it. The route hadn't made sense. That was why the statement sounded wrong. 'When you gave your statement, did you say you left Lian by the bull?'

'Of course. Why?'

'Just checking the facts.'

Back at my desk, I searched the system for Mei Li. Nothing came up. I went back to Lian's file. The investigating officer was Mike Weatherall. Died of cancer the following year. It was probably his last case. There were two big murder investigations at the time. Most of CID, including me, was on one or the other. Mike was left to keep the remaining wheels turning. He must have tampered with Amy's statement. I didn't know how. More important, I didn't know why.

I rechecked the notes for anything that could answer that question. Finally, I found a cross reference tucked away in the back. I looked it up. It was Mei Li. It had been misfiled on the system. Another anomaly. The case was closed six months before Lian went missing. The investigating officer was Mike Weatherall. It was too late now to collect the file. I put in a request and headed home.

The rain outside was biblical. It overwhelmed the drains and settled in pools across High Street. Shoppers ran into each other, trying to avoid them. By the time I reached the bull, my clothes were too wet to hold any more water. It was dripping off me. I'd seen a lot of that statue since moving next door to him. He's a landmark. A place to meet. I circled him and thought of Lian Chen waiting to meet someone. Someone that made her happy.

I went into the Rotunda, my building, left a puddle in the lift and let myself into the apartment. I dropped my keys next to hers, changed clothes and found a coat. I switched myself on to repeat mode and left for Kimmie's. A few hours later I returned home, wet again, and sat on the couch in the dark with my pal, JD.

The reason whisky is my sedative of choice is its ability to knock me out cold. I don't dream. Or, rather, I don't recall dreaming. That night, it let me down. I dreamt I was back outside the apartment, that damn chain locking me out. I called her phone and heard it ringing inside. I shouted to her. I banged the door. I threw myself against it and woke up to find myself on the floor.

It was still dark. Except it's never really dark in that room. The city is always outside. Illuminating everything it touches. I stood at the windows, contemplating how easy would it be to open one and step over the rail. I got a grip on myself and returned to the safety of the couch.

I was about to sit down when I noticed a green light, like phosphorescence, in the window. It was the size of a tennis ball but was growing before my eyes. Forging itself into a shape. A face. *Her* face. For a second, I thought it was a reflection. She'd come back. I turned around. There was just me. I swivelled back again. She was gone. I launched myself at the windows but it was useless. She wasn't coming back. I was half asleep. I'd imagined it. I slid to the floor and buried my head in my hands.

The weightlessness of Mei Li's file surprised me. It was the thinnest I'd seen. I placed her photo next to Lian's. Lian was a pleasant looking girl. Neither pretty nor plain. Whereas Mei had the kind of face you'd remember. Neat, perfectly symmetrical, with big eyes. I felt I knew her. Maybe I'd seen her around back then.

The file didn't take long to read. It took longer to process the shock of what it told me. Mei Li was last seen in her Rotunda apartment by Lian Chen. The same apartment where I now lived. I checked the investigator. Mike Weatherall.

'All right, Ash?' Tony Ryan stood over me. He was the DI in charge of Salina's case.

I covered Mei's notes as casually as possible. 'Sorry, Tone, didn't see you there. Bit bogged down.'

He sat on my desk. 'Got you clearing up the shit, has she? I expect she told you we're scaling down? Sorry mate. It's out of my hands.'

'It's okay. I get it.'

'No hard feelings?'

I shook my head. Something occurred to me. 'Tony, do you remember Mike Weatherall?'

'Yeah. Nice bloke. Good copper. Why do you ask?'

'I'm looking at one of his cases. It's a bit sketchy.'

'Not like Mike. He was pretty thorough. Want me to take a look?'

'No, you're fine. It's mundane stuff. It was 2012. I expect it was the illness.'

'That'll be it.' He walked over to a nearby window, 'I fucking hate rain.'

I let him go without showing him the file. I don't know why. It could have helped with Salina's case. Maybe it was the shock of finding Mei had lived in our apartment. Maybe it was because I recognised a name in there.

I shook the rain off my coat. Sat in my usual seat. Gave my usual order. Kimmie brought the drinks over. 'Any news on Salina?'

'They're scaling down the investigation.' I could have told her that the night before. I'd tried but the words wouldn't form. This time, it wasn't such a problem.

'What does that mean?'

'They're close to throwing in the towel.' I watched her reaction. If she was shocked, she didn't show it.

'What'll you do now?'

I shrugged. 'I don't know. What did you do after Mei went?'

She raised an eyebrow. For Kimmie, that was the closest to surprise you could hope for. She was one cool individual. To the point of icy sometimes. I never got what Salina saw in her.

'I got on with my life, like you should.'

I winced, 'She was your daughter.'

She corrected me, '*Is* my daughter. She's still alive.'

'You sure of that?'

'Absolutely. Salina is too. They'll both come back when they're ready. You just have to choose whether to wait for her or not. Me? I'm waiting.'

I leaned forward. 'Why didn't you tell me or my colleagues about Mei?'

'They didn't ask. Anyway, it's already on record. They just needed to look.'

'And the apartment. Why didn't you say something before we moved in?'

'Salina already knew.' She stood up.

I grabbed her arm. 'Both Mei and Salina disappeared from the same place. You knew, and you kept it to yourself. Why would you do that?'

She pulled away. 'Mei didn't disappear. She just left to be with her father. Read the report. As for Salina? Nothing I could say would help. Now, you still want your food, or you leaving?'

I threw down some cash and walked.

I took the same route as Lian. When she left Amy, she had to have been going to our apartment. What was it about that place? I kept on walking, past my building and up New Street. I didn't know where I was going. I just knew I had to walk to think.

Before she disappeared six months ago, I'd known Salina for three years. But how much did I really know her? Why didn't she mention Mei? My brain replayed scenes from our past. Anything that might point to something I'd missed. I started with the apartment. Rented through an agency. She'd organised it. I just signed on the dotted line. Next, her family. She said she didn't have any to speak of and I didn't question it.

When I reached St Paul's Square, I turned back. I needed to go home. I had to find out more about her. And, I was soaked to the skin again.

When I got in, I pulled off my wet clothes and took a hot shower. But three days of rain is hard to shake off. The dampness clings to the flesh and softens the bones to aching. I made a fresh pot of coffee. I needed the warmth, and a clear head.

The Crossing Place

Her passport and other ID were at the station, but I was searching for more than that. The tenancy agreement was in the drawer where she kept important papers. I found the landlords and looked them up. I didn't need to.

I checked her drawers; wardrobe; clothes; her desk. I upended furniture and turned the place over. Not one single personal detail. I was back on the couch. No further forward. I switched off the light and bedded down. But, when you've just consumed a potful of coffee, sleep doesn't come easy. So, I lay in the dark, doubts of all kinds whirring around my head.

It must have been a couple of hours later when I heard it. No more than a whisper.

'Ash.'

I sat up and scanned the room.

'Ash.'

I followed the sound, towards the phosphorescent shape. A blurry image, juddering and flickering, like an ancient movie scene. The same as the one that had appeared in the window the night before. Except that it wasn't in the window. It was on the other side of it. It was outside. Hovering. Eighteen floors above the ground.

'Ash. Come to me.'

'Salina?'

The window felt cold and hard as I pressed against it. I shut my eyes. If this was another hallucination, then let it burn into my retinas and stay there. Something warm touched my cheek. Something soft and tender. My stomach lurched. I opened my eyes and moved slowly away, fearful of what I might see. Mei Li's face was staring straight at me. Not from outside. It had somehow become part of the glass. I was so fixated, I didn't register the hand reaching through until it had mine. I panicked and jerked backwards. It held me in its grip. It was thick and strong. Definitely a man's. I reached for the nearest thing, an empty bottle, and smashed it against the bare skin. It let go and shot back into the darkness. Mei's face melted away. What had I done? I spread my hands around the glass, manically feeling for some sign of life. Nothing. Just solid, unyielding glass. I was going mad. No other explanation for it. I sank to my knees and cried like a baby. I couldn't help myself.

I stayed awake all night. The rain finally stopped at dawn. A grey haze formed a canopy over the buildings. A chink of sunlight found its way through and settled on the window, highlighting a streak of red on the glass. Dried blood. I examined myself. No cuts. So, the arm had been real? Not mad then.

When I got into work, the Danish on my desk reminded me I hadn't eaten since yesterday lunchtime. I threw it down and set to work on tracking Salina's background. There were plenty of official records for her. But they all stopped seven years ago. To put it another way, she didn't exist before 2012. I guessed Tony Ryan knew this too. He probably had her down as an illegal immigrant. She would have hated that. She once lost it with me because I suggested she had roots in Asia. 'Why? Because I have brown skin? Have you presupposed my religion too?' It pissed her off when assumptions were made based on someone's skin colour, race, gender - or lack of. Or pretty much anything. She was the only person I knew who seemed to be entirely without prejudice. She was more woke than woke.

By lunchtime, my stomach was doing somersaults. I got myself some proper food for a change and switched my research to Mei Li. The case conclusion was that she'd gone to her father. His address in Hong Kong didn't exist.

Other than Mei's birth certificate, there was no further detail on him. I'd come to a dead end again. I finished up early and went for a beer with my team. They seemed pleasantly surprised. On the way home I bought a ready meal.

The smell of beef and noodles hit me as soon as I opened the door. She was in the kitchen putting the food onto plates. 'I've brought dinner to you. As you've stopped coming to me.'

I flashed my carrier. 'I've got a ready meal.'

She shrugged. 'It'll keep. No chopsticks?' I shook my head. She tutted, cleared the junk from the table and put the plates down. 'You responsible for this mess or did someone break in?'

I handed her some cutlery, 'I was looking for clues.'

She stuck her fork in the beef. 'You won't find anything.'

'I found out you're my landlady.'

She snorted. 'No offence, Ash, but if you only just found that out, you must be a pretty shit policeman.'

She had a point.

'Why are you here, Kim?'

'To ask you to drop the case. It's not what you think. And because Salina asked me to look out for you.'

I sucked air through my teeth. 'If Salina asked you to look out for me, that must mean you both knew she was going. Where she is?'

'You wouldn't understand.'

'Try me.' She ignored me and picked at her food. I was getting nowhere. Time for some honesty. 'I've been seeing things. In the window. Images. Salina and Mei. I know this sounds crazy, but last night, an arm came through that window.'

She dropped her fork. I had her full attention now. 'Salina's? Mei's?'

'No. It was a man. I'm sure of it. Kim, you have to tell me. What the fuck is going on?'

'Did you see the inside of the wrist. Were there any markings?'

I concentrated and visualised the whole crazy scenario. The face moulding itself into the glass; the arm reaching out from nowhere. The arm. Think about the arm. Yes. There had been a small tattoo. 'Some kind of symbol, on the inside of the wrist. Like a sailboat.'

'Do you have a pen and paper?' I found some. She drew a kind of Chinese junk boat. 'Like this?'

'That's it.'

She took a lighter from her bag, stood over the sink and lit the paper. 'It's Kai. Mei's father. Tell me exactly what happened.'

I recounted the details of the last two nights. When I finished, she poured us both a drink. 'How long has your family lived in Birmingham, Ash?'

I shrugged. 'On my mum's side? Forever. Dad's was a mixture.'

'Mine have been here since 1960. People thought we came from Hong Kong, but they were wrong. We were much closer than that.'

I sighed. She was leading me down another blind alley. 'What's your point?'

She ran her fingers around the rim of her glass. 'Wherever you look in this city, there are traces of the past. Echoes of another time. But what about other times, other cities? Do you believe it's possible to have echoes from the future? Or even an alternative present? Other versions of this city sitting alongside this one.'

I laughed again. She had to be shitting me. She wasn't smiling. Fuck. She was serious. 'That's crazy. How would it even work?'

'I don't know. It just does. I don't even know how many versions or timeframes there are. I just know they co-exist. Few cross between them. My parents did. They settled here. I grew up blissfully unaware, until Kai showed up. He crossed over in 1987. I fell for him and got pregnant with Mei. But he didn't like it here. Too gritty. Too small-minded. You name it, he hated it. He stuck it out for a while, then went back. He wanted us to go too, but I refused. So, he went alone. But he returned, now and then, to fill Mei's head with stories about this better place of his. Like it was some kind of Utopia. The last time was 2012. He took her back with him.'

'And Lian?'

'Lian was a complication. Poor girl was besotted with Mei. Mei must have told her everything. She threatened to go public. I had to let her cross over. I have no idea if she got to Mei. There are no communication lines and the crossing places don't always align.'

'What about Salina? Was she from this other city?'

She nodded. 'She and Lian crossed together, in opposite directions. She arrived by accident. Something to do with her work. All those calculations. She's been trying to return ever since. Meeting you kind of stalled things. She loved you, Ash.'

'She still left me.'

'She had her reasons.'

'I would never leave her.'

'She had a child. The pull was too strong. I know what that's like.'

'She had a child?'

How could that be? Surely, I would have known. She would have trusted me enough to tell me. And if it was true, there must be a father too. Who was this woman I'd shared my life with?

'Yes, but if she's here, Ash, she must need you pretty bad.'

I wasn't listening. I was thinking about Salina. I'd have done anything for her. Stood in front of a moving train if she'd asked me to. I thought what we had was honest. I couldn't have been more wrong.

Kimmie was still talking. 'She promised she'd find Mei and she's done it. They've come for us. We can join them.'

'Join them?'

She grabbed me. 'You're not listening, Ash. If they're at the edge of the crossing place, it must be aligning. It could be years before it happens again. If we want to, we can be with them.'

I shook myself free, 'Why would I do that? She lied to me.'

'Because you have nothing here to keep you, and she needs you. This other Birmingham. It's not the paradise Kai thought it was. Salina told me. It has its own problems. The sort that make ours look insignificant. She lied for your own good. She crossed back to bring her child to safety. If she's come for you, she must be in trouble. At least wait with me until I cross over.'

'You're going?'

She nodded. 'I want my daughter back.'

It was past midnight. We were side by side on the couch.

'Is it always here, in this building?' I asked.

'No. There are crossing places all over the city, but this one's strong. My dad discovered it in the seventies and rented an office here. I bought this when they repurposed the building. I knew Mei would go eventually. I wanted somewhere for her to return to.'

'Something else I can't work out. Where does Mike Weatherall fit into this?'

'Mike was my friend. More than that. He covered up Mei's disappearance when Lian reported it. Then he helped with Lian. He knew he was dying-'

She broke off and pointed outside to the green light glimmering like a new-born star. 'They're here.'

The nearer it got, the bigger and brighter it became. It bounced off the glass until it took form - that movie image again - and pressed through. Salina's face in 3D. Her eyes darted around the room until she found me and her lips parted into a wide smile. In spite of everything, I smiled back. Right then, I knew I'd still stand in front of that train for her. And if I had to cross worlds to do that, so be it. I loved her more than my own life. Nothing else mattered and anyhow, honesty was overrated.

With my eyes still fixed on Salina, I said to Kimmie, 'I'm going with you.'

The arm emerged from the darkness. A distant male voice called, 'Hurry. It won't hold for long.'

Kimmie's hand slipped into mine. She was shaking. 'I'm afraid, Ash.'

'So am I. Don't let go until we're through.'

I reached out my free arm. The hand closed around mine and I felt the pull of a magnetic force.

I looked out at the city one last time. It was beautiful.

SECOND THOUGHTS
By

C.P.Garghan

The key slid into the front door lock and I tried to calm my racing heart as it began to turn. When the lock clicked and the door swung open, I let myself gasp a sigh of relief. The driver's license in my wallet had led me from the hospital to this flat looking out over the concrete flyover in the heart of the city centre, but I had no idea whether it was up to date. Still, I pushed my way inside and memories began to emerge: a loose jumble of familiarity and associations from which I could piece together the layout of the flat. A narrow corridor led into a combined living room and kitchen; on my left were two doors. The first was the bathroom – I remembered that much – but the second was… another bedroom? My flatmate's perhaps? On the right was my own room. I pushed open the door and felt a wave of relief as I was greeted by the familiar Ikea bed, the shelves groaning under the weight of books crammed into every surface, and the glass tube of a lava lamp.

'Localised lacuna amnesia' the doctors had called it: a short-term failure to recall certain facts and details from memory. They had tried to test me for it at the hospital, but after weeks of eating dry chicken, over-boiled vegetables, and tasteless jelly, I had resolved to leave the ward, regardless of any short-term memory problem. A few carefully concocted lies and educated guesswork had convinced the fussing doctors and nurses that I was safe to re-enter society.

Second Thoughts

I emptied the bag of clothes into the washing basket and made my way into the living room, trying to see whether the surroundings would trigger any more memories. Dominating the middle of the room was a minimalist grey sofa with cushions badly in need of replacing. I ran my hand over it and shuddered; the last thing I remembered before being taken into hospital was lying on it, feeling a tingling in my limbs, the dense knot in my stomach, and the ringing in my ears which preceded a seizure. In the corner of the room was a television stand, its surface given over to a collection of candles and a radio ever since the television was removed to try to prevent the epileptic attacks. I tried turning the radio on, but my head was in no mood to hear about 'football coming home.'

Tea. That was what I needed, I told myself, and made my way into the kitchen to fill the kettle and pull a carton of UHT milk from the fridge. Clearly, somebody had expected me to be away for a while, but who? The kettle clicked. I found the teabags and poured some warmth to settle my jangled nerves. With warm mug in hand, I settled on the sofa and tried to piece together what I knew, what I thought I knew, and what was still lost beyond the fog of the operation. I knew my name, where I lived, certain names and faces of relatives and friends; I was pretty sure that I knew where I worked as an… accountant? Clerk? I was vaguely confident that I did not live alone, but any further details were a mystery to me.

I set the mug down on the coffee table and walked to the door of the other bedroom, but when I raised my hand to open it, I hesitated. Was this an intrusion? What if they worked nights? How would I feel about somebody just making their way into my room? I let my hand drop from the handle and returned to the sofa.

Whoever I lived with, they didn't believe in keeping the fridge well-stocked, so I set about making a shopping list and finding practical things to do to keep my mind away from the hazier areas of my memory. By the time I had filled the fridge, cleaned every surface within an inch of its life and eaten, the sun had begun to set and my bed was calling me. I glanced at my flatmate's bedroom door, and considered knocking again, but something held me back. Instead, I found a block of yellow post-it-notes beside the telephone and wrote a quick message:

> *Got back from hospital today,*
> *Still feeling rough,*
> *Going to bed. Will see you tomorrow (?)*

With that, I stumbled into my room and was asleep before my head hit the pillow.

It could have been hours or days later when I finally awoke, but the first sensation to hit me was the throbbing in my skull, another side-effect that the doctors warned me could be coming. What they didn't warn me about was the dry mouth that tasted like an ashtray. I groaned, pulled the covers off, and plodded into the bathroom, stopping only to pop a couple of high-dosage painkillers from the hospital bag.

Opening the bathroom door gave me a little more insight into the behaviour of my unseen cohabitant. The toilet seat had been left up, suggesting a male flatmate, and a towel sat in a soaking heap on the floor. The towel itself sparked a nebulous familiarity: I knew its multicoloured stripes well, so perhaps leaving it on the floor was a common occurrence? Sighing, I picked up and folded the towel, closed the toilet, and re-arranged the cluttered shelf before carrying on with my own ablutions.

I showered, dressed, and made my way into the living room to start the day and felt my shoulders drop. The

Second Thoughts

coffee table was strewn with empty and half-crushed beer cans, some festooned with dog-ends of hand-rolled fags.

How had I not heard him? I wondered as I set about collecting the remains of the six-pack and straightening the cushions on the couch. I threw open the windows to air out the smell of stale smoke and tried to remind myself that I didn't know anything about this person, that it wasn't fair to resent somebody you didn't know. Perhaps this was just a one-off occasion? Niggles in the back of my mind told me it wasn't.

I put up with the stabbing headache pains as I threw the empty cans into the bin, a part of me hoping that I would wake the person responsible. Who went out and got drunk when their flatmate was still recovering from brain surgery? Who would deliberately leave the place where they were going to recuperate a mess? Had he even seen the note I had left?

I glanced over to the telephone table and saw another note beside it. So, he had seen my note then. Perhaps this was an apology?

No apology: instead, the paper was covered in intricate doodles, every square inch of it filled with stylised birds breaking out of exploding cages, rigid geometrical patterns dripping and dissolving into swirling loops and clouds. It was a thing of beauty, but not an explanation for the chaos of the flat, so I scrunched it into a ball and sent it to join the empty cans and fag-ends in the bin.

I picked up the pen left beside the telephone and wrote another note:

> *Cleaned up the flat,*
> *Going for a walk to clear my head.*
> *Maybe talk later (?)*

The air of the city centre was hardly fresh, but compared to the stale fug of the flat, it was like a sweet mountain breeze. As I walked, details began to fall into place. Little memories which had skittered away as the light of my recollection fell on them held still long enough for me to grab them. I worked in a large accountancy firm in the business district; I remembered taking my lunches out to Pigeon Park. I found the pubs I used to drink in, the favourite little restaurants. So why were the details of my home life so flimsy?

As I made my way onto New Street, my breath caught in my throat and I instinctively raised a shaking hand to a healed scar just behind my left ear as the memories of a particularly bad seizure came flooding back to me. I had been shopping and the day had been bright and sunny; perhaps it was the light of the sun shining off the buildings, perhaps it was the dappled light through the summer trees, but I remember feeling the world drop away, my ears beginning to ring, and the jolt of pain as my head hit the corner of one of the decorative planters. By the time I came around from the seizure, I was already bundled up in the back of an ambulance and being sped to Heartlands Hospital. It was while recovering from the head trauma that doctors first discussed the surgery which would lead to my current amnesia.

I ran my hand along the corner of the planter, considering how this unassuming piece of street furniture had so radically changed my life. If it had been placed a few inches one way, hitting my head against it could have killed me; a few inches the other and I would have missed it entirely. The architect who had designed this layout would never have any idea just how significant a few lines on a plan would be.

My head hurt: all the memories and recollections cascading down on me at once were overwhelming.

Second Thoughts

Reluctantly, I turned around and headed back to the flat to spend another day slowly recuperating in a darkened room.

The next day, I woke up feeling fresher than I had felt in weeks. The walk yesterday had been good for me and a solid, uninterrupted sleep had worked to knit together some of my broken memories. I was in such a good mood, that I didn't even mutter to myself when I found the living room again in a state of total disarray. Instead, I was fascinated by the guitar lying amidst balls of crumpled paper. I sat on the sofa and ran an experimental finger along the strings of the guitar. The sound brought back loose but happy feelings of recollection, as though the sounds of the guitar had been a source of happiness before the amnesia.

With a smile, I began to pick through the balls of paper. They were all covered in a scrawl of illegible writing until he had clearly given up and had instead sketched ideas with abstract cartoons instead.

Even without my memories, I was beginning to get a sense of my otherwise invisible companion. I pictured him sitting on the sofa, strumming along on the guitar and perhaps humming along, not to rigid words or notes from a score, but beautiful doodles and artwork. I wished I had been awake to hear him play.

I collected the bundles of paper, straightened them out and gathered them up to take them to my room. I couldn't bear to just throw them in the rubbish. I noticed that the note pad beside the telephone had been moved again and my note had been replaced with a picture of a face pulling a thoroughly apologetic expression and a cartoon of an empty bin, complete with shining sparkles. I turned around to see that the bin had indeed been emptied and the kitchen left spotless.

Thanks for tidying, I wrote on a new note.

> *I wish I'd heard you playing last night.*
> *Feel free to wake me next time.*
> *:)*

I leaned the guitar against the radio and carried on with my day. At lunch time, I jumped at the sound of the phone ringing.

'Hello?' I said.

'Hi, this is Eddie from the office, just calling to ask how you're getting on?'

Eddie. The name sent an immediate shudder through my being. He was a line-manager so incompetent that it wasn't a surprise he'd be phoning somebody who'd only been out of the hospital after major surgery for a little more than a day.

'Hi, Eddie,' I said. 'I'm back at home, at least. The hospital said that the side-effects of the surgery should start to go down over the next few days.'

'Right, right,' he said, evidently trying to push the conversation to his point. 'So, when do you think you'll be back at work?'

I laughed. It wasn't deliberate, but I just had to laugh at the sheer brass-neck of him.

'Eddie, do you know what a *corpus callosotomy* is?' I asked. 'It's where they peel your skin back, crack your skull open, and slice through the bit of your brain holding the two hemispheres together. At the moment, I'm having trouble with my memory, my balance is all over the place, and I've got – literally – a splitting headache all the time. No, I don't know when I'll be back at work.'

There was a pregnant pause on the other side of the phone.

'Right.' Another pause. 'So, we won't expect you back soon, then?'

Second Thoughts

I put the phone down. For a moment, I luxuriated in the kind of rebellious thrill that would come as natural to somebody who would spend their nights drinking, drawing, smoking, and playing the guitar.

Days passed and memories slotted into place, until the only gaps concerned the fascinating individual that I lived with. On the first day after the phone call, I found a tape left next to the radio. When I slotted it into the machine, I found myself listening to a home recording of the guitar. Old rock and punk hits played on an instrument built for classical ballads; the combination was intriguing to listen to.

The notes and drawings got increasingly elaborate and soon they filled my cupboard door with everything from funny cartoons, to incredible inked masterpieces, as though the artist was trying to express everything and didn't care about consistency or creating a single voice.

He performed and created while I slept. Sometimes, I found cans left discarded around the flat; sometimes, there were cigarette butts pushed into mugs and glasses. Every time, I cleaned up after him and wondered how I could possibly have slept through it all.

Although my post-operation self had never met him, I began to piece together his character through the clues he left and the contrasts with my own personality. I tended to cook simple meals, keeping the kitchen spotless as I went about the process of preparing food. In contrast, I would sometimes walk into an explosion in the kitchen, with pots and pans everywhere, packets of ingredients left open and both the bin and fridge filled with the results of culinary experimentations. I listened to the same radio stations and filled my recovery with reading books; he listened to everything from the hits on the BBC to pirate stations I'd never heard of. I left out copies of classic books by Stephenson and Mary Shelley to read, while he left copies of the NME lying on the floor.

We left each other notes to find, like ships passing in the night. I complained about his untidiness and he'd leave me an apologetic drawing and leave the flat clean(er) the next day. He would leave behind art that I would spend the mornings drinking up, whether that was recordings of tunes or sketches left in books or, increasingly, paintings of everything from landscapes to surreal abstractions.

I hadn't met him, but I think I was falling in love with him.

He was everything that I wasn't. I was methodical and organised; he freely embraced the chaos around him. I spent my time with words, reading them, writing to myself, or listening to Radio Four; he seemed to almost entirely eschew anything as predictable and understandable as words. He and I, two worlds drawn together on either side of a small block of yellow sticky notes.

One night, I decided that I would finally meet him. I poured myself a strong cup of tea, brought a heavy book into the living room and sat up until the streetlights burned yellow and the daytime traffic of commuters and shoppers outside became the night-time world of revellers and taxis. The tea was drained, filled, and drained again. I put down the book and tuned into the radio. The shipping forecast came and went, and Radio 4 gave way to the World Service, I felt my eyelids getting heavier and heavier, and my nerves increasingly strained.

Rationally, I knew that it wasn't fair. He didn't *know* that I was staying up to meet him, but a part of me felt like there was a connection between us, that somehow, he must *know* that I was waiting to speak to him. The clock on the wall ticked over from one to two to three, the sky began to glow with the pale blue light of pre-dawn, and I found myself stalking the flat like a wild animal.

Second Thoughts

In that lonely early morning, all the frustrations I had spent days carefully packing away along with the dishes and cutlery came crashing down in pile after pile. Why hadn't he been there for me when I had come out of hospital? Why had he left me to come home to an empty flat? Why couldn't he just pick up his god-damned towel off the floor? Why did he always leave the place looking like a pigsty no matter how many times I *told* him how much it annoyed me?

And why couldn't he speak to me like a normal human being? Suddenly all the cute cartoons and intricate drawings annoyed me more than they made me smile. How much effort would it be to just write a quick note?

I stormed into my bedroom and grabbed the wall of post-it-notes I had been building on my cupboard and started tearing at them like a man possessed. I didn't care if they ripped or came away whole, I just wanted them gone. When I was finished, I collapsed on top of the yellow snowdrifts that I had turned my bedroom floor into and ran my hands through the hair which had started to regrow.

The sun rose, the city woke up, and my flatmate still hadn't shown up. Through gritted teeth, I made my way back into the living room and wrote a terse note beside the telephone.

> *Waited to speak to you.*
> *Guess you were out.*
> *Speak soon.*

Afterwards, I picked up the phone and dialled a number I hadn't planned on calling until the doctors had given me the all-clear.

'Hi Eddie,' I said. 'I just wanted to say I'm feeling a lot better and I'm ready to come back into the office.'

C.P. Garghan

My days back in the office started well, Eddie, for all my own animosity towards him, worked hard to make sure that I had support coming back into the swing of things – taking on small accounts to start off with and giving me a couple of junior team-members to help out once I started to regain the larger projects.

For a few days, I didn't see any evidence of my flatmate. I assumed he must have gone away on one of his creative whims. At first, I felt a pang of regret about not getting his little notes when I woke up, but I had to admit that having a clean and tidy flat was a satisfying relief.

It was only after a week or so on the job, once routine had started to kick in again, that he returned. At first, the only difference was his sketchbook left on the sofa, or his guitar left leaning against the wall. I took it to mean that he must have realised that I was back at work and was trying to make things as easy as possible. Soon, the cans returned, along with the cigarettes and the mess and the increasingly elaborate art pieces. Work suffered too, his antics giving me poor nights' sleep which made focusing in the office a challenge.

After a day where I'd woken up and spent half an hour cleaning before nearly falling asleep at my desk, I decided I'd had enough.

I let the heavy door slam behind me before I loosened my tie and dropped my bag in my room. I found myself staring at his door, some part of my brain screaming at me to leave it alone, to walk away and just leave another note beside the telephone. I glanced into the living room: the post-it-notes were empty, the pen lost somewhere to an art project. I drew in my breath and knocked on his door. Once, twice.

I stood in the hallway, feeling my stomach inexplicably turning somersaults – why was doing something as ordinary as knocking on my flatmate's bedroom door filling me with such dread?

I knocked again, louder this time. When he didn't answer, I knew that there was only one option left to me. I placed one hand on the door-handle, felt the cold of the metal running through my skin, and began to turn.

The handle clicked and the door swung open.

Despite the amnesia, I had always known that I had the larger room. His was an internal room, the only light coming from a borrowed light window set high up by the window, and it was small. Until I opened the door, I hadn't realised how small.

It was a cupboard, that was the only way to describe it. A single camp-bed with no pillows or blanket occupied half of the floor space; the rest was filled either with boxes or instruments, easels, and the dusty television I had removed from the living-room when the epilepsy had become too bad.

I frowned and backed out of the room. This didn't make sense. I looked for anything which could give me some idea about the man willing to live in such a cramped shoebox, but besides a heavy camcorder and other assorted odds-and-ends, there was nothing. It was as though… no…

I thought I knew him, perhaps not his name or what he looked like, but I *knew* him. I knew what he liked, what drove him. What's more, I knew how he felt about me. Even when he was being selfish, it was just his disorganised mind at play, I thought about all the songs he'd recorded that he knew I enjoyed, the paintings which caught the light *just so* as I walked into the living room in the morning, and yet this was not a space in which anyone lived. It couldn't be.

I went to bed that night with my mind racing. Tomorrow, I would have to find answers.

The next day, I woke with my head buzzing with ideas. I would find our rental agreement, call up the phone company and find some numbers I could call to piece together the mystery. I'd dedicate my time to going through the boxes in the other room.

I would find out who I had been living with.

All the plans were thrown into chaos when I opened the living room door and saw a videotape lying on the sofa with a note attached to it. On it were two words in the inimitable, jagged and clumsy style of the man I thought of as my flatmate.

pLaY ME

The old television had been set-up in the corner of the room, its screen hastily and ineffectively wiped clean of the layers of dust and grime which had built up on it. Frowning, I pushed the tape into the built-in VHS player and sat back on the sofa.

The tape began to play to reveal the same sofa I was now sitting on. The camcorder had been set up besides the telephone. As I watched, a familiar figure walked from behind the lens to sit where I was sitting now.

'Hi.'

My mouth dropped open as I watched a perfect doppelganger of myself run a nervous hand through hair identical to my own. He looked up to the ceiling and took in a deep breath to steady himself, it was a nervous tic that I recognised in myself. 'I'm guessing by now you must have worked out what's happened. There's no shame in how long it took you, especially since I was the one gifted with the imagination in our relationship.'

He – I – he smiled nervously, like a teenager trying a cheeky joke on a first date.

'It was the operation, of course,' he said while he balled his hands into fists and brought them together. 'The surgery cut the link between the two hemispheres of the brain; stopped the two sides from interfering with one another to stop the seizures.'

He split his fists apart and held his left up to the camera, as though presenting me with something.

'The left side, largely responsible for language, logic, all that boring stuff – you – and the right side, in charge of creativity, imagination, the stuff that makes life, well, worth living.' He clenched his right fist close to his heart. 'Me.'

'Usually, we're both active at the same time, both contributing what we can to the other; now only one of us can be in charge at any given moment.' The me on the screen reached a shaking hand for a can of beer just out of frame and brought it up to his lips. 'That first night after we got home was terrifying. I had never been fully in charge before, never had to navigate both sides at the same time. You have the language centre; you've got the words to express what's happening to you. It's because of language that you've been in the driver's seat for so long. I didn't have the words to say what was happening: all I could do was to try to express myself however I could.'

I shook my head and pinched myself. This had to be a dream; it *had* to be. What else could explain this?

'When we went back to work, I tried so hard to stay silent, to give our body the rest it so desperately needed, but I couldn't do it forever.' He looked up at the screen, a look of determination in eyes that were unmistakeably mine. 'I shouldn't *have* to do it forever. This body, this *life* belongs to both of us, equally. All our lives we've been an unknowing team, echoing one another, reflecting each other back at ourselves.'

He leaned forwards, a fierce sparkle of determination in his – my – eyes.

'This is me, no longer the echo.' He held out his hand towards the camera, reaching out for me. 'Reaching out to you.'

AWAKE
by

Kirsty Handley

'Please,' Mila pleaded. 'I'm only a little bit short. I really need this. I work so hard, but by the time I've paid for food and rent, there's nothing left.'

The woman on the desk at Birmingham benefits centre gave a sympathetic smile and gestured to the long line that had accumulated behind her. Whilst she understood Mila's plight, she had heard it all before, with each desperate murmuring of a recipient behind the glass dulling the generosity of her human spirit. She was early on in her career and still had some small reserves of compassion for the endless tales of suffering and hardship, but it was the computer algorithm not her that had the power to decide which was the most deserving.

Mila consequently shuffled her feet towards the door, glimpsing the desolate faces on her exit. Desperation was apparent everywhere she looked; hard luck stories as common as the sunken eyes and weary bodies. Nobody was loud enough to make their grievance openly heard. They might lose their much-prized place in the queue and even a tiny bit of hope was better than no faith at all. Instead they muttered, as if singing the same desperate and desolate melody, hoping that somebody had the ability to change the tempo and the key.

Mila's body felt terrible and every limb ached with an excruciating numbness that started at the tip of her head and stretched down to her very toes. As she put one foot in front of the other, she made a shameful retreat from the centre, with nothing to show for four hours of queueing. Her own eyes burned like small fires in her sockets and the fog in her brain was gaining momentum, cocooning itself around any coherent thoughts. The rain felt somewhat refreshing, a light downpour on an August day. Whilst it could not revive, it was at least partly invigorating and, best of all, it was free.

She arrived at the bus station. There was nowhere to sit down and every second she was forced to stand, she felt the painful aching of every nerve in her legs and back. She waited thirty minutes before finally clambering on and lowering herself down onto a seat. She looked at a newspaper someone had tossed aside. The words were spinning on the page, refusing to form anything that she could realistically decipher, but eventually it revealed a headline – 'The end of scrounger Britain' – with Sebastian Jackson, the Prime Minister, smiling smugly in his expensive, tailored suit and perfectly white teeth, standing in an overly confident pose that she could imagine he had practised since the age of seven. She knew the sentiment. It was one formed on social media accounts and parent forums in leafy and green suburbs, by people who never had to worry where their next meal was coming from, or whether the lights might suddenly go out because the electricity card could not be topped up. These were people who would never worry that their jobs would be swept from under their feet after many years – unlike those who were expected to share the pain of a recession without having seen the rewards of a boom. For those who were lucky, zero-hour contracts were the substitute with the opportunity to sit around all day praying that the phone rang. The less fortunate received a quick muttering of thanks as the door closed behind them, with just two weeks of pay to show for it.

Awake

This was a narrative that was absent from this realm of middle England opposition. Articles were liked and reshared, decrying lazy and work-shy people, occupying accommodation that they had not paid for, whose sole activities were watching television and playing violent video games whilst drinking and chain-smoking all day, purely at wealthy taxpayers' expense. Sebastian Jackson had been elected on a mandate of doing something about it and for that reason, in some homes and gardens across the country, he deserved the title of national hero.

Mila remembered that traumatic and awful day in the cold and airless medical surgery with its sickeningly cheery, yellow walls. She was number seven hundred and three as she waited for a computer-generated announcement to release her from another queue. Yet unlike a typical day at the benefits centre, this was a landscape that rippled with loud objections.

'It's a disgrace,' an old man said angrily.

'They can't do this. How can they make refusal a criminal offence with a prison sentence?' an old lady shrieked.

'Do they understand the effects? What if it goes wrong?' a teenager said dramatically.

The people around her acted as if by stating these sentiments, they could wrestle some level of control back over their own lives, but the receptionist on the counter looked bored and the passionate protesters knew it was futile. Ultimately, it was not going to change the outcome, no matter how vociferous their objections, or how many tears they managed to summon.

When it came to her turn, the doctor had been officious, believing that all power came from the electronic tablet he held in front of him. 'Thank you for coming,' he had said insincerely – as if she had been given any choice.

She refused to even dignify him with a response. The prick in her skin caused little pain, at least in the short term, other than a brief yelp. The doctor gave her a plaster and a fake smile, then she was on her way.

For the next few weeks, television programmes were interrupted by government adverts, her favourite songs on the radio destroyed by commercials, in local supermarkets, or anywhere she chose to frequent. The message was simple: Get your sleeping tablets in all good stores. Work hard and pay for them, to reverse forever being awake. One dosage a night will give you the best sleep that you will ever have and earn your right to rest. It seemed designed to crush any opposition. People who argued against it were fanatics and lunatics, on the fringes of the political spectrum and a danger to your children. How could people who had barely even completed science classes at fifteen hope to compete with the brightest minds in the country? Anyone with a degree, who might actively have thought of opposing, was given an ultimatum that they would never practise science again. The truth was presented as simple: this was not an opinion; it was merely a fact.

The first time she had visited the supermarket had been terrifying. With an inevitable shortage of tablets, people swung elbows, feet and anything else they could use to knock fellow shoppers out of the way in mass hysteria to get hold of some. They stockpiled baskets and trolleys with the ring of the tills barely able to move them through quickly enough before shelves became bare. Fingernails scratched other wrists, and in the single-minded mission for a good night of rest, it did not matter if it was friend, neighbour or family member. Yet being able to sleep did not negate the need to eat. Mila had left the store with one carrier bag containing a box of cereal and a few cans of Red Bull – all she could afford with the resources at her disposal.

She arrived at the sleep bank, all set for another painfully slow line. It was a dilapidated building with few hints at its former glory, but she was prepared to swallow her pride and hoped that nobody recognised her or registered the shame clearly plastered across her face. Alice, one of the volunteers, was just coming out of the door and locking it behind her. 'Can I help you?' Alice said gently, obviously not recognising her, which was surprising given that Mila had fastidiously being visiting every fortnight.

'I was hoping for a pill,' Mila said, despising the self-pity in her voice. 'I just feel terrible. Work is exhausting, you know.'

Alice looked at her with a sad smile. 'Ah, haven't you heard? We're closing now; all the banks are going. The government couldn't afford to keep us open. I'm really sorry,' she said gently. 'Have you tried the benefits centre?'

Mila tried to hide her exasperation when she replied, 'I've just come from there. They said they couldn't help,' as a tear ran down her cheek.

'I'm sorry, there's just, there's nothing we can do. This is becoming a boutique hotel,' Alice said sympathetically. Her concern was genuine, but it would not solve any of Mila's problems. 'Don't you have any family, friends who can help you? I know it can be tricky to reach out.'

Mila thought of Luke, the one her mother would always have loved. Solid and dependable Luke who had never done anything reckless in his life. He had not stopped calling and texting her for weeks on end, even appearing outside her front door a handful of times. He had sent large bunches of flowers, handwritten letters –

deliberate and considered, numerous texts and voice mails, with the clear desperation of one who believed something had to be the key to reconciliation. He had even written her a poem, which she had promptly tossed straight into the recycling bin, without even taking the time to decipher its contents.

When Luke held Mila in his arms for the first time, she perhaps felt safe. She finally had something to hold on to that was secure and would not slip through her fingers as everything else seemed to have done previously. Yet whilst Mila was determined to make her mother proud, the compromise of safety over passion had felt a heavy burden to bear. When describing Luke, the two obvious adjectives were pleasant and nice, but she felt there had to be something more to life. Then she found the form that he had carelessly left lying around on his kitchen table, for employment as an administrator for the vaccine scheme.

'What's this?' she had screamed, the carefully cultivated, nice girl persona that she had spent months perfecting to keep hold of him evaporating in an instance.

'It's for us, Mila – a better future. The pay is great – we can put a deposit down, move somewhere better,' he had volunteered as his eyes portrayed how startled he was at a girl he did not recognise.

She glared at him. 'How could you, you traitor? You're disgusting! In league with them!'

'In league with who, Mila? It's for the best. They're the government and they know what they're doing,' he said almost smugly, which enraged her. 'Do you want to live like this forever? Like your mum, working all your life, then just drop down dead? Forever having nothing? Scrimping for cash?'

The dilemma Mila had about whether a future with Luke would ever be truly capable of making her happy ended abruptly. Too full of anger even to speak, she had simply gathered up her bag and walked out of the door, slamming it for good measure as she left. The sense of liberation was unexpected. The soft and gentle role she had been forced to play as his girlfriend was exhausting with the need to constantly hide the sharp edges. How dare he mention her mum! She had told him that in a moment of weakness. He was dating a fantasy and she had terminated her acting contract.

'No, there's nobody,' Mila muttered, and off Alice went to kiss her children good night and swallow a pill before settling down on her luxury body-sculpting mattress. Alice would remember Mila's face for a while, but it would eventually fade. Her children's school would need someone as a parent governor and she would throw herself enthusiastically into her new duties as her days at the sleep bank became a distant memory.

Mila felt a faint buzzing as if there was a permanent swarm of bees following her and they were becoming more vicious as the black fog in her brain intensified. She knew they were not real, but if the start of insanity was hearing things that were not there, this was a worrying development.

She finally returned home to her tower block. It was a dilapidated building like the ones Prime Minister Sebastian Jackson had promised his new taxation on sleeping tablets would serve to help. Yet if the project was on the regeneration list, it was very low down. It seemed that the government believed people who were tucked away in flats had the benefit of being out of sight and mind, no matter how terrible the accommodation they were forced to live in. They had a home and for that they should be grateful. The only professional workers who came here were the police and even they preferred to stay away. Few people visited and an even smaller number ever left the block for something better.

'Hey, Mil.' Mila looked up and saw her little eleven-year-old neighbour Nasreen calling out. Nasreen was waving a picture on her phone, in front of Mila's face. 'Can you recreate this? I love the colour,' Nasreen said excitedly.

Mila looked down at the photo then half smiled at her wearily. 'Ah, I'm sorry, Nas. I'm just shattered.' Mila was not convinced she had the strength to hold a brush, let alone have the delicacy for the lines needed to recreate the bright glittery butterfly on the Instagram model's face.

'Ah, okay, no problem, don't worry. Sorry for asking. Hope you're okay,' Nasreen said good naturedly, but the disappointment on her face broke Mila's heart more than what had awaited at the job centre and sleep bank.

'Mum and Nilesh are at it again,' Nasreen said quietly, looking around, nervous to be telling tales on her family.

'What about?' Mila said gently. Nasreen's mum and her boyfriend Nilesh seemed so wrapped up in each other, they almost forgot Nasreen was there. How that could be perplexed Mila because if she could have had a little sister, she struggled to think of anyone warmer and kinder than Nasreen.

'Mum thinks Nilesh is cheating on her,' Nasreen blurted out.

'Is he?' Mila said more sharply than she intended.

'He went out a couple of nights ago, didn't come back for ages. I don't know, Mil; they're always yelling at each other. She went mad when he did the washing up wrong the other day. How do you do it wrong? Is this what a relationship is supposed to be like? I don't want a boyfriend.' Nas pulled a face and looked confused for a second.

'You don't need one. Listen, I promise I'll do the butterfly tomorrow.' She gave Nasreen a brief smile and the girl wandered off. Mila took a deep breath and opened the door to her flat, ignoring the guilt she had felt over sending Nasreen away. The situation in Nasreen's home seemed ever more volatile, but Mila was just not sure she had the energy to do anything about it.

As she walked into her flat, she nearly tripped over the job applications, chucked all over the floor, that she had printed from the local library. The government was looking for applicants to occupy a variety of positions as part of the new high-speed rail project and international sports competition that were coming to the city. However, alongside exam qualifications and previous experience, alertness was an absolute necessity. She knew that she was lucky to have the cleaning job, but it barely paid for the copious amounts of energy drinks needed to successfully complete the endless cycle of repetitive rubbing, washing and dusting. The local council did not want zombies as a showcase for the city; it was not good for its public relations campaign. Her frustration had resulted in her throwing them on the floor, then despairing at her idiocy that she would have to tidy them up again.

She remembered the last interview she had had. She had stood in another line as she waited to be let into a soulless room. Applicants had been given basic instructions or so you would have thought. Click your mouse instantly when you see hazards. However, the lack of sleep had dulled her senses and she failed to acknowledge the sheep crossing the augmented reality road or the motorbike that had appeared from nowhere. She had bowed her head as an angry message in red proclaiming 'fail' had appeared on the screen. The fake look of pity on the tester's face, as if she had never seen anyone actively not pass before, stayed with Mila long after she had returned home. Mila had thought she could beat it using energy drinks, but there was a drugs test for those these days. The government argued it was to level the playing field and promote personal responsibility.

Mila ignored the mess on the floor and collapsed into a heap on her bed. Should she just go for it? Beds fetched good money and whilst it was beautiful, it was currently very redundant. She could put the earnings towards pills which would last for a couple of weeks. Yet with the sofa long gone along with most of the rest of her other furniture, the cold floor was not enticing in wakefulness or in sleep. Lying on the soft mattress cocooned by cushions would not simulate slumber, but it was the cheapest and closest thing to it.

An aggressive knock at the door ended this trail of thought and she opened it. In walked Tom, looking dishevelled. His baggy, grey hoodie was stained and the bags under his eyes looked almost as dark as bruises. 'Hey baby,' he slurred.

Mila pushed him hard. 'Where have you been? Get away from me! I gave you some money and you never came back!' she yelled.

'I was only gone for a little bit,' he countered in that lazy drawl she had once found so endearing and now disgusted her.

'It's been two months and I hear nothing!' she shrieked.

'Money's kind of gone.' Tom was intuitive enough to convey some awkwardness. 'I was just so tired, you know, and I...'

Mila rapidly interrupted him. 'You were tired; you were exhausted! It was my money and you spent it – on sleeping pills, I'm guessing.'

Awake

'I've got some stimulants,' he offered, almost as a peace gesture, 'The best the estate has to offer.'

'Get out!' Mila screamed now. 'Never come back, you selfish waste of space!'

'Mils, I'm sorry.' He was begging now, but it only served to intensify her rage. She realised he smelt faintly of perfume and it was not a brand that she recognised. If he had not been in her flat for two months, it was unlikely he had spent the whole time on the street. She felt nauseous thinking about it.

She shoved him out aggressively, slamming the door, and sat on the floor for a while, head in hands, tears streaming down her face. She couldn't believe his last words to her had been to ask for his stimulants back. She knew whilst he might be gone for now, it would not be forever. It was confusing how you could love and despise one person quite so much. Even ten years on from the day that they had met at school, she still found him intoxicating and she had been naturally attracted to his innate confidence and how he seemed so sure of everything when she herself felt so lost. She had once simply revelled being in his company, feeling as if he liked her for who she was rather than a character she had to create as with Luke.

Every now and then, she managed to convince herself that they could write a new chapter and discard the previous pages, no matter how tainted. He was always keen, happy to play the central character in a tale of redemption, but it never lasted. Tom might still be a toxic narcissist on eight hours of consistent sleep a night, but she realised that it was unlikely now she would ever know.

She had trusted him with that money, thinking it would be a test. He had gone for two nights of sleep for himself, rather than one tablet each. When push came to shove, no matter the circumstances, he would always put himself first, despite the proclamations of love that dripped so easily out of his mouth. She was sure he believed them at the time. Yet he existed very much in the present and the narrative was consistently evolving, according to what was most favourable to his own interests. When Mila aligned with these, it created a high she could not replicate with anyone else, but it was never permanent, and every rejection chipped away at her self-esteem.

The cheap stimulants felt good and she tried not to think about the inevitable come down as she sat staring outside the window. Stimulants had become hard currency on the estate. She hated fuelling the local drug related violence and loathed the fact people like her were part of the problem. Yet another night sober, watching the clock tick past, was just too painful to contemplate. The stabbing envy could be all consuming towards any quiet neighbouring flat whose occupants had reached utopia at least for one night. Number sixteen had been silent for a little while and she tried to ignore the jealousy she felt when she wondered if perhaps its elderly inhabitant was having a night of peace.

Mila went to the kitchen drawer and got a knife out. The vicious bees in her head were aggressively looking for an escape channel and perhaps if the pain on the inside transferred to the outside it would make it better. She traced her veins on her arm with the blade of a knife. How far would she have to go before she was given a friendly set of paramedics, a cosy hospital bed and a nice sleeping tablet? It would be Utopia for one night; a pause on all her problems. She continued circling her arm with the tip of her knife, the thoughts becoming more real. *Do it*, the inner voice was saying. *It's the only way to get what you want. Everything will just get better if you're not so tired.*

Suddenly there was a bang on the door and Mila shot up, repulsed by this sudden foreign object in her hand.

Awake

What was she doing? What if she had done real damage to herself?

'Go away, Tom. Leave me alone!' Mila shouted. Although Tom always tended to make a hasty return, it was rarely this quickly: he was manipulative enough to leave the red fires of her anger to fade before he dared to return.

'It's me. Sorry, Mil. I didn't want to disturb you I just wanted to get out of there.' Nasreen was gently sobbing so the words were muffled and difficult to decipher.

Mila let her in, and Nas stepped into the flat, wearing her pink pyjamas and dressing gown, fluffy slipper boots on her feet.

'What happened mate?' Mila said gently.

'Ah, they're just at it again, screaming the place down. Nilesh went for Mum. I think they're both too tired. I was scared. I shouldn't have left her there, but she won't leave. I went in between them, but Mum told me to go and leave them to it.'

Nasreen looked guilty now and she was shuffling her feet on the floor.

'Your mum should be protecting you, Nas, not the other way around. Are you hurt?' Mila asked anxiously.

'No, I'm fine, just...' Nasreen looked embarrassed now. 'Just a bit hungry. I haven't eaten since yesterday – there's no shopping in the house. I think it's what started it between Mum and Nilesh.'

Mila gave Nasreen some cereal and let her eat, a companionable silence forming between the two of them.

'Do you have any sleeping tablets?' Mila asked inquisitively.

Nasreen mumbled, 'No, it's always tricky in the summer. We get them free at school but not so much in the holidays as the services aren't really open. Do you have any?' Nasreen said brightly.

'Sorry, no,' Mila muttered. 'You can stay here, though, whilst they calm down a bit. We can just sort of chill and rest before I go back to work tomorrow at four a.m.'

Nasreen nodded.

'You're safe here,' Mila continued.

'Why do you work at four a.m.?' Nasreen asked and then blushed, realising that it was an intrusive question.

'Ah, those people in the offices think that they are self-cleaning. The ones with their expensive laptops and designer handbags,' Mila chuckled. 'They imagine their rooms dramatically become clean and we wouldn't want to destroy the illusion.'

They both started giggling at the stupidity of these people and their laughter warmed the August night-time air, at least for a short while.

Mila and Nasreen lay on the double bed, willing sleep even though they both knew it would not come. As a little girl back when dreams were free, Mila had imagined being a makeup artist. She'd longed for the ability to transform something ordinary into something exceptional, replicating all the colours of the human emotional spectrum. She didn't care if it was the theatre, the catwalk or just ordinary girls with big dreams to look special; it did not matter if she had a brush and a palette of colours in her hand. Yet the only time she used those skills these days was to disguise the dark circles that plagued her eyes, which was necessary to hold on grimly to her cleaning job. Instead of contour and highlighter brushes, it was sweeping floors and scrubbing worksurfaces. It was now about surviving and putting one aching leg in front of the other.

The voices in Mila's head were getting louder as the stimulants began to wear off, to be replaced by all-consuming exhaustion once more. This was replicated throughout the tower block and in bedrooms across the country. Harassed mothers worried how much they were bawling at their young children as they struggled to even find time simply to have a shower. Parents struggled to keep their teenagers in the house, terrified at how much trouble they could get into during the additional hours under the cloak of darkness. Couples broke up and got back together on a regular basis between screaming and softened tones as they balanced the need to occupy endless lonely nights, with the irritation of being locked in a small space together with little money to do anything else. For those lucky enough to have a radio and television set, they were turned to full volume as if to remind their audiences that they were not the only person awake and other people were sharing in their suffering.

Exhausted people will do desperate and irrational things. Sebastian Jackson's sleep injection had spurred people to action, just as his supporters had brayed for. Yet it was not the action that he had foreseen and as he lay in a peaceful slumber on his luxury four poster bed, he had no idea of the ugly nightmare that was to come.

THE UNWRITTEN STORY
By

Rachel Parkinson

Chapter 1

Sitting in the coffee shop, watching the first beads of rain hit the window, her hands holding the warm cappuccino bowl, was a luxury for Lily. It felt comforting as she settled into the leather armchair, taking the first hot mouthful to her lips, drinking longingly and savouring the aroma of fresh coffee and hazelnut.

Glancing around the shop to see if there was anyone she knew, she could see it was fairly empty despite the rain. It was still too early before the post-five o'clock customers piled in. Lily was relieved; the past two weeks had been difficult. Dealing with the death of her Great-Aunt Lillian and supporting her father throughout that time had been a strain. She needed some time to herself.

After finishing her training course in the city centre a bit early, there was no rush to get wet just yet, she thought. Peals of thunder could be heard across the gloomy sky. The condensation on the windows acted as a barrier to the outside world, dulling the intrusion of the noisy, busy city. Lily felt safe in the cafe and oddly comforted by the thunderstorm.

Being alone at her table meant she inevitably began to catch up on her emails from the past week on her phone. There was another email from Pearson & Harlow, the family solicitors, probably for her father where she was copied in, but the start of this email seemed different to the others. It was addressed to her personally, marked as urgent.

The solicitor was asking her to attend their offices at her earliest convenience, tomorrow if possible, accompanying her father for the reading of the will.

Damn, she thought, she hadn't realised it was tomorrow. Returning her father's phone call with an apology for being so busy, Lily agreed to be there when the will was read. The email had described an envelope that her great-aunt had left for her, to be opened by her in the event of her great-aunt's death. Maybe it was the details of a piece of jewellery or a rare book that she had been bequeathed, she thought. With a sigh at her empty cup, it was time to dodge the storm and head for home.

The offices of Pearson & Harlow were in one of the old Victorian buildings in the city, on a street that had traditionally housed solicitors and bankers over the years, in the Colmore Row area. Their office was no exception: the room smelled of old books and polished furniture, with a more recent hint of good coffee. The sunlight beamed through the window blinds, dust particles slowly dancing in its rays. She thought of all the people who had passed through these offices over the years; some with high expectations, others leaving disappointed.

Lily was curious to know what the envelope contained, but conscious that her father was feeling the weight of the moment. He had been a favourite nephew of his aunt and had in fact been the only one in the family whom Lillian had been very close to towards the end of her life. Although married for a large part of her life – her husband passing away twenty years previously – she had had no children. Lillian had been fond of her nephew, and proud when he had named Lily after her. Lily had met her a few times when she was a child and then as a teenager, and had heard some stories from her father about the work that her great-aunt did during World War 2. She was learning more about Lillian as the days elapsed after her death. Lillian had been 100 years old when she passed away peacefully in her own home. Being away at university and then starting her new job had kept Lily busy over the recent years, with little thought for the passage of time.

The solicitor, Mr Pearson (one of the many Pearson juniors to work in the company through the years), was friendly and reassuring. Even though this was his business, he had known Great-Aunt Lillian, and seemed genuinely concerned.

'Morning John, Lily, please take a seat', said the solicitor, gesturing his arm towards the seating.

'Thank you,' said Lily's father, acknowledging the courtesy but not wanting to make too much small talk.

Mr Pearson responded with a smile as he attempted to get down to business and offered them some drinks by way of a distraction from the conversation. Shuffling papers on his desk, and looking at something on his computer, he began to explain the will.

Great-Aunt Lillian had left her property and a respectable amount of money to Lily's father, some details about smaller gifts for other relatives not requested to be present today, and a sizeable donation to the British Red Cross charity. Finally, for Lily, there was an amount of money and a list of Lillian's personal belongings, including some books, which she had been bequeathed.

'You mentioned an envelope?' said Lily, looking nervous but not wanting to appear too eager to know what it contained.

'Ah yes, the envelope,' said the solicitor, looking through an old folder on his desk. 'This is the envelope addressed to you, Miss Lily Atkin, to be opened in the event of Miss Lillian Atkin's death, as were her wishes.'

He passed the envelope across the desk, looking at her with a smile, and asked her to record the receipt of the item with a signature.

Lily looked down at the envelope, written on the time-old quality Basildon Bond brand. Just thinking about Lillian writing her name evoked a feeling of sadness and regret. She knew she had to wait until she was alone before opening it. Lily looked at her father, her expression conveying an apology, and placed the envelope in her bag.

Chapter 2

Lillian's house was a 1950s style building with a large bay window at the front, rose bushes in the small garden and a row of smaller conifers lining the boundary to the neighbour's property. Lily knocked and walked in, looking for her father.

'Hi, Dad. I brought a flask of coffee and some biscuits. I didn't think there would be anything here for us to use. Hope you don't mind?' Lily said as she walked through the hallway looking up the staircase then turning left into the front room. Her father stood at the fire surround with his back towards her.

A table and four chairs sat empty in the window area, a linen tablecloth draped over it with a notepad and pencil in an empty crystal fruit bowl. She imagined her great-aunt sitting there, people-watching, looking out for the postman, writing her shopping list, the school children passing by and the sound of their laughter echoing in the air.

'I hadn't thought of that. Well done,' said her father. 'I was just looking at this clock, thinking about how many times I've sat here talking to her, hearing the ticking of the clock but never really noticing it until now, in this empty room,' he reflected – and now she wasn't there anymore.

'Well, let's have a drink and see what we need to do. If Lillian was here, she wouldn't want us moping around. She'd want us to get on and get things done, I'm sure.' Lily tried to comfort her father, giving him a brief kiss on his forehead as she spoke.

'Yes, I suppose so. I've got a list of things I need to go through, paperwork and stuff. I'll sit here and make a start. You go on and have a look around.'

Lily poured the coffee and placed the mugs on the linen tablecloth, careful not to spill a drop.

'Did you open the envelope? What did she say? Was it jewellery or her medical books? Perhaps have a look around upstairs, maybe in her bedroom,' suggested her father.

'No, not yet. I was waiting to do it here, in her home; it seemed like the right place.'

Lily reached into her bag for the envelope and headed upstairs.

Great-Aunt Lillian's bedroom hadn't been touched since her death. The bed was made and the room kept clean, although Lillian had slept downstairs on a single bed since she had become ill. Her room was how she had left it, more or less, with Lily's father and assorted carers and cleaners doing laundry and keeping the rooms dust-free over the past few months.

Lily looked around the room, taking in the details of the furniture, the writing desk by the window, the pictures and photos on the walls, the ornaments and belongings arranged in a special way. Things that had been cherished by Lillian, sending back the sound of the past. The room had been waiting for someone to explore, to touch, experience and consider the memory behind each trinket. Here there was a lingering essence of Lillian: rose scent perfume and talcum powder, personal items on the dressing table. An imprint of a life fully lived.

In this room, Lily felt calm and quiet. She sat at the desk and opened the envelope. What she read made her feel like an intruder in her great-aunt's life:

My dearest Lily,

You were named after me, your Great-Aunt Lillian, your dear father's aunt, whom you probably can't remember much about, as you were very young and I was already old.

I have watched your progress over the years, listened to your father's praise of you as he told me how well you did in your exams, and then how proud he was of you for getting your job at the hospital. I was proud too and wished I could have spent more time with you, but my recurring illness prevented that, and you were away at university.

I wanted to give you a gift, to remember me by and to make up for lost time. I have instructed my solicitor to give you my jewellery, which was my grandmother's, so it is only right that this is passed down to you, Lily.

I have also given Pearson's a list of my books and journals of the time I worked at the Queens Hospital. These are now yours. You will find them in the right-hand drawer of the writing desk; the key is in my jewellery box.

Now I come to the important part. I am asking you to do something for me, Lily – something that I couldn't speak to your father about, which really needs a woman's touch. I know you will understand when you read what I ask of you.

Lily had read to the end of the first page. Her eyes were full of tears but they didn't fall, not yet. She sensed that Lillian was there, speaking to her, her presence felt in every little detail of that room. She looked up, almost expecting to see her, but her glance fell towards the photos on the wall. Some were of Lillian; one of an attractive man in a suit, her husband presumably; and possibly others were relatives unknown to Lily.

She felt nervous as she turned over the page to read the rest of the letter, glancing around for the jewellery box.

I don't have much time left, and my strength fails me as I write. Look in the desk drawer and find the diaries and papers I refer to. See they are the beginnings of a story: of my time spent at the hospital, of the people I met; a record of my life.

I want you to finish that story, Lily. Take all my notes and diaries and finish the work I started. You will find everything you need in what I have left you, and in your own heart, I am certain, Lily, you can do this for me.

Take the time you need but hear my warning: don't waste that time when it comes around for you.

With much love and affection,
Great-Aunt Lillian x

Tears flowed down Lily's cheeks as she read the second page. The ache she felt for someone whom she hadn't known well but now missed was heavy in her chest. She needed to compose herself in case her father should come upstairs and find her sobbing over her great-aunt's letter like this. She dabbed her face with the back of her hand and moved towards the jewellery box, searching for the key to the desk. Lillian had some beautiful pieces of jewellery, and Lily smiled as she admired them sitting there, all for her, special memories for Lillian that were now bequeathed to her to treasure always.

Lily opened the desk drawer and picked up the bundle of papers and books that had been kept together with ribbons to keep the loose papers secure. Laying them all out on the desk, she realised the weight of the task before her.

The Unwritten Story

It was the beginning of a biography: scraps of text written on old paper. Then there were annual diaries from when Lillian had started her nursing training until her retirement, some with the usual diary entries of reminders and appointments, others with paragraphs of writing. Some letters were addressed to Lillian, bound with another ribbon. All these things documented a journal of her life.

'Where on earth do I start, Aunt Lillian?' Lily said out loud, half expecting to get a response. The tingling sensation creeping up her arms made the hair stand upright. She suddenly felt cold and alone. She re-read the last part of the letter.

'Take the time you need but hear my warning: don't waste that time when it comes around for you.'

What did she mean by a warning? Lily gathered all the papers and diaries, closed the door and went back downstairs.

'Hi, Dad, you were right. Lillian did leave me her jewellery. I'll take it with me when I come back. Are you going to be here tomorrow? I'll come by and take it then, if that's okay?'

'Sure, just take what you need, in your own time. The house won't be sold just yet,' he said.

'What are those?' he asked, looking at the bundle of books and papers under Lily's arm.

'Oh, just the journals from when she worked at the hospital. She asked me to take care of them and thought I might be interested in reading them sometime.' Lily played it safe, not wanting to arouse his curiosity any further. Thankfully he hadn't noticed she'd been crying.

'Ah, so that explains her letter. She was a nurse, then a matron, you know, during the Second World War; I'm sure she touched many lives during those years.' Her father was proud of his aunt and of what she had achieved in her lifetime as a nurse at the Queen's. 'I might have a few old photos for you, if you remind me. I'll see what I can find.'

'Thanks, Dad, that would be great,' said Lily, thinking how the photos would be another piece of the puzzle that Lillian had left for her to solve.

Chapter 3

Chatting briefly about the situation with her work friend Jill had resulted in more questions but moved Lily towards a starting place. It was all well and good reading a few journals and papers, but how to piece them all together was the stumbling block as some of the papers were not even dated. Jill had suggested creating a timeline, documenting everything into a chronological order, then making a separate list of any questions that arose, where information was missing, or dates and years had been left out. That way it wouldn't feel like such a mammoth task. To Lily, it already was a 'mammoth task' in her mind, but also in her heart; she had already made a promise to Great-Aunt Lillian to try and achieve her wishes.

'Have you actually written anything other than your medical dissertations? Or an autobiography, which is what this will be now, I suppose?' asked Jill, curiously.

'Not really; I could do the work when I needed to, for my medical degree, but actually writing about an unknown subject for someone else who's not here to read it is a first for me.'

'So, a bit of a challenge then?' said her friend. 'Although not such an unknown subject; your aunt worked at a hospital didn't she?'

'Yes she did, so I suppose that's something,' said Lily.

'Why don't you try the library or the museum? Maybe someone there can point you in the right direction if you give them a few details,' said Jill.

'It's a worth a try, I suppose. That will be really useful, thanks, Jill.'

They got back to their paperwork, before their shifts started again.

She decided she needed to know more about the Queen's Hospital, despite what she could learn on the internet. Delving into the archives and finding out more about a real place would hopefully answer some of the questions she was starting to ask herself. She had started to read through Lillian's notes every day – and every night, as it turned out.

Chapter 4

Lily stood looking up at the red brick and stone building of the old Birmingham Library, now known as the Birmingham & Midland Institute (BMI). Acting as a guardian to this city of echoes, its history resounded to each new generation to walk along its streets. The Victorian façade reflected the years of learning and knowledge it contained within its walls. After a chat with a couple of staff and a walk around the rooms, leafing through a few books and articles, what detail they had given her would be useful in its own way. Lily was disappointed not to have found as much as she thought she would; upon reflection, thinking it was all going to come together after a couple of hours there, she had been mistaken. The commitment she had made and the sheer quantity of Lillian's legacy reminded her it was a big undertaking. She focused her mind and headed for the Birmingham Museum and Art Gallery. The new library could wait for another day.

Lily tried to remember the last time she had been at the museum. When her family had visited she had taken them on a tour of the city, the best known places for the tourists, sticking to the streets she knew and where she felt safe. Ignoring the temptation to sit in the Edwardian tearooms, Lily headed straight for the history exhibitions on the third floor. The wartime display had always interested Lily: there were so many layers to interpret, lest we forget... The exhibition was small, but the focus was the same: resilience and courage. Even the museum had become a survivor. The shades of green on the uniforms blended into one, but a single colour remained: the red cross, symbol of hope in a crisis. Lily stared at the display, thinking about Lillian and trying to imagine what she must have experienced as a young nurse in a damaged city, dealing with patients broken and disillusioned.

Thinking about Great-Aunt Lillian living through those war years, she knew training as a nurse in the 1940s must have been difficult: Lillian would have realised she was being trained to deal with the emerging tragedy to follow in the war, not fully understanding it all and the trauma that would impact so many lives.

Someone was standing nearby watching her expression. She could see his reflection in the glass cabinet and turned around suddenly, conscious of her eyes brimming with tears.

'Oh, I'm sorry, you just seemed so interested in this exhibition. Did you have any questions? I'm Daniel,' he said, holding out his hand. 'I look after this exhibition, well the whole floor really.' He seemed friendly and smiled, looking expectantly at Lily.

'Sorry, er, yes, I was just thinking about a relative,' she said, returning the handshake.

The Unwritten Story

'Someone who fought in the war? Which one?' he asked curiously.

'Nothing like that, although I'm sure there were, but, no, I was thinking about my great-aunt who was a nurse at the Queen's Hospital in World War 2.'

'Oh 'The Acci'? That's what us Brummies call it, but yes it was the Queen's Hospital back then. I think it's student accommodation now – it's had a few changes over the years,' he said.

'Yes, probably,' she replied, looking at him fully now. 'I've not been there yet: I'm looking into the history of the city during World War 2, and my great-aunt's connection to the hospital; just doing some family history really,' she explained, not wanting to tell the real story to this stranger, despite how friendly he seemed, not to mention interesting to look at.

Daniel began to provide some useful facts, all the while also now fully looking at Lily with her smooth skin and sea-blue eyes. He was keen to help: that was his job. He had a lot of knowledge that would be helpful to her, he was certain of that.

'If you've got time now,' he said, 'I could show you some of our archives. There might be more information that could help.'

He was very helpful, she thought; maybe a little too interested, she smiled to herself; but this was an opportunity to learn more about what she needed to know, if she was ever going to make a start on Lillian's story.

'That would be great, thanks. I'm sure there will be something I can use for my family history,' she said shyly.

'Great! Let me just let my colleague know I've made an appointment for you now, and we can start some research. Do you know exactly what you're looking for? Or is it a bit vague, like family history can be sometimes?' he asked, as they walked through a staff corridor towards the archives office.

'I have a few facts and some gaps. I think I need to know a bit more about nurses during the 1940s for a start, and anything you have about the hospital would be helpful,' she said, trying to stay focused on the reason she had come to the museum in the first place.

Daniel seemed really nice, very friendly and not pushy like some men had been in the past. Some of them had been so pushy in fact that she had backed off completely and kept herself busy in her studies and now her job, which she had allowed to fill any spare time she seemed to have lately. So, two hours later, Lily left the museum with a slight spring in her step, and a lot more than she had bargained for: Daniel's phone number for a start, and a follow up invitation to 'discuss details again, over coffee.'

Chapter 5

'Yes, I got his number, Jill,' said Lily on the phone to her work friend, who had asked about how it went on her day off. 'Well you can tell me all about it next week when you're back in,' she said. Lily could hear the laughter in Jill's voice as she hung up.

Now time to call Dad, thought Lily. 'Thanks for the photos, Dad,' she said. 'They're great, and I've managed to find a few details about the hospital where Great-Aunt Lillian worked, so now I just need to find time to read those medical books she left me.'

'That's great, sweetheart; you might learn a few things that they couldn't teach you at that university of yours,' he said cheekily.

The Unwritten Story

She sat on the floor of her spare room, papers and diaries spread all over, in order of years, with some photos overlaying them, next to a few open books she had borrowed from the library, and some handwritten notes from her chat with Daniel. Daniel: yes, she would need to call him as she had a few gaps to fill... Lily closed her eyes and pretended Great-Aunt Lillian was in the room again. 'Again, Lillian, I ask you: where do I start?' She didn't really expect an answer, but something felt like a voice inside her head saying, 'Start at the beginning, obviously.' Of course, at the beginning, of Lillian's life as a nurse, when she started her training at 18 years old, just like Lily when she started her medical degree. A few hours later, with more notes written down and papers rearranged on the floor, a few more cups of coffee and a hungry yawn, Lily felt she had started to make some progress.

What she hadn't expected to discover was that Lillian had loved and lost – just like so many people during the war years who had lost their loved ones to the tragedy of the times, which had shattered hopes and dreams for a golden future, to be slowly pieced back together, like a jigsaw with no picture to follow. The bundle of letters had revealed a romance between Lillian and another member of staff at the hospital, but no explanation as to what had happened, or who he was. Lily felt like she was intruding into Lillian's private life by reading those letters. Sitting up in bed until 2am, tears slowly rolling down her cheeks, she felt overwhelmed with sadness.

This revelation in her great-aunt's life was a surprise. Lillian had been married for many years, and her husband had passed away when Lily was a little girl, so she hadn't know him. Her father had known him by his nickname, Champ. The flow of the script showed a writer who was deeply in love, that was clear from the longing he had tried to express in words. Lily felt a little embarrassed to be reading them. They had been part of what Lillian had left her to piece together, so would need to be read and re-read if Lily was going to do any justice to the story of Lillian's life and love-life. The enormity of what Lillian had experienced in her early life began to unfold, still with some missing pieces in the jigsaw of her life.

Lily had arranged to meet Daniel again and talk through her next chapter in the 'family history project'.

'That sounds incredible, to be given such a personal insight into your great-aunt's life,' he said. 'It's her private life in some respects, but then also she asked you to write her story from all those notes.'

He was surprised but intrigued to know more about Lillian and the historical connection to World War 2, and started to think about how he could put more 'life' into the exhibition he was responsible for.

'Yes, it is incredible,' she said, her face animated at the sheer task before her. 'But that she should ask me to do it, and that I should even think I can bring it all together! I have no idea how long it's going to take, but I know I have to do this, for Lillian.'

They continued to chat about some of the missing details and Lily took comfort in knowing that Daniel now shared this task and could help her in some way. She knew she would have to explain to her Dad what she had found, at some point, but it could wait a little while longer.

Lily reflected on Lillian's warning from her letter: 'Take the time you need, but hear my warning; don't waste that time when it comes around for you.' Lily knew what she meant, that time was now, here with Daniel. Thinking back to the love letters, Lily wondered what had happened with the young man who had poured out his heart to Lillian when they were just starting their careers. She thought of how the war had affected their lives and separated them, presumably. She knew she needed to continue her task, for Lillian's sake, even if it took much longer than she had expected at the start. A promise was a promise, after all.

A few months later, as they walked hand in hand along the pier at Brighton, Lily gave thanks for Lillian's warning. She had allowed herself to trust again, and was now enjoying a short break with Daniel, who had gently persisted in seeing her and helping her with her 'story'. But it was more than that, though: this was a new beginning, a new chapter in her own life.

'So are you definitely going to write the story?' asked Daniel as Lily's gaze drew back from the foamy waves of the shore to the dark blue of his eyes, his smile...

'Yes, I am. I'm not sure what kind of writer I will turn out to be, but I made a promise to my Dad that I would try, and to Lillian too.'

'Do you know who the man was, in the letters? Did your aunt mention him at all before she died?' Daniel was curious to know, but conscious not to tread too heavily on Lily's feelings.

'Yes, I think I do. It's been becoming clearer as I've been able to piece some of the dates and events together, spanning quite a few years. I need to talk it over with Dad first, before I start to write him into the story. Apparently, Dad knew him when he was young, by a nickname, but he died twenty years ago...'

'Well then, that's where we'll start, when we get home.'

'We?' she asked, as they stopped briefly, heading back along the pier towards the shore.

'Yes, we can write the next chapter together,' he said, folding his arms around her as the waves ebbed and flowed against the tide.

Reading the love letters again, Lily had seen now that every one of them had been written in the same hand and they had all been signed, 'With all my love, Champ.'

REFLECTIONS
By

Mohammed Rizwan

I first saw him on the walkway of the Grand Union Canal at Anderton Rd, Bridge 90. He was looking at his reflection in the water and brushing his hair. How he managed to see anything clearly in the dirty waters, I have no idea.

I looked away as I passed on my way to the bridge at Coventry Rd. It was my default action for dealing with weird people.

'Who brushes their hair in canal waters?' I asked Maria as we sat in a café later.

'Canal waters?'

'Yeah, especially those ones. So dark and dirty. How could he possibly see anything?'

She sighed, looked at the newspaper, and asked, 'Anything in there for me?'

I turned to the job listings and scanned waitressing roles.

'I've told you, Maria, to look up. You'll never get anywhere waitressing.'

She took a bite of the chocolate cake, chewed, and took a sip of the coffee.

'Waitressing has been good to me. Good for me.'

I rolled my eyes, safe behind the pages of the paper. Waitressing has never helped anyone. Maria was too clever to be in a job that used her legs and not her brain but she refused. I get so anxious, she would say. Anxious at what? Having to use her brain?

'Ooh, here's one. Oh, how odd. It's at the café at Bridge 90 where I saw that man!'

'That man sounds crazy,' she said, snatching the newspaper. 'Do I really want to work there?'

I didn't respond. The man had been dressed in a suit. Maybe he'd been in a hurry and didn't have anywhere else to check his reflection. He seemed like a city person. Bridge 90 Café had been set up a few months ago by some hipster neighbours, so it seemed unlikely he would visit.

'What can I get you?' Maria asked me, looking all coy, pretending she didn't know me. I played along.

'Can I get a croissant and a pot of tea, please?'

She took the order down (could she really not remember something as simple as that?) and smiled, saying she would be back in a tick. The café was heaving. I'd never taken this canal walk on a Saturday afternoon, so hadn't realised it would be so busy. I'd hovered at this table for a good twenty minutes. The occupants had pointedly looked at me, their eyebrows raised but I wasn't Maria. I returned their looks with equal ferocity until they left.

I turned my face to the sun, eyes closed, and basked, grateful for these outside tables. If I could turn into an animal, I'd want to be a cat. Sleeping in the sun for twenty-one hours sounded like a dream. I sighed and opened my eyes, gasping a little at the sight of a man standing behind the other chair, grasping it.

'So sorry to bother you,' he said, 'but can I sit here? There's no other seats free and I'm dying for a cup of coffee.'

The other day, I hadn't seen him full on, only his profile, and I was suddenly glad. If I had seen his full face, I don't think I would have been able to look away – something that was happening now.

Reflections

His burnished hair glowed, his eyes reflected the perfect blue of the sky, his strong chin called me to touch it, his rounded cheeks begged to be caressed. And his voice. Music. Not that modern disharmony. It was as if the perfection of mathematics and physics were reified into this sound that I was sure would stay with me for all time. Some part of me chimed, clinging to his words' assonance, clinging to his words' consonance.

All thought was lost and I saw his image in all the corners of my mind.

My thoughts were broken by Maria's return. The man was still looking at me. I cleared my throat.

'Yes, of course.' He smiled and the world stopped again, his white teeth blinding me, forcing me to look away, towards Maria, who was also entranced. She held a tray, her hands gripping it so tight it seemed the blood had stopped there.

I took the tray from here and set it down, moving the little vase with the daffodil out of the way, while he sat and asked Maria if he could order. He asked again at her lack of response. I kicked her.

She nodded and took out her little notebook.

'A coffee, black, no sugar, and some water, please.'

She nodded once more and scrambled away.

I couldn't look at the man again. If I did, I knew I'd embarrass myself, so I prepared the tea, adding a sugar cube and a dash of milk, but I hadn't let it steep enough and I grimaced at the first sip.

I looked at the man over the rim of my cup, only to find his head was bent, looking at his phone. I lowered my cup and saw that he was looking at the front camera app, at his own reflection. Strange.

He looked at his face, this way and that. He was beautiful but did he need to call attention to it? He looked up suddenly and smiled. I didn't have time to look away and bit my lip while smiling. I probably looked constipated.

'Sorry.' He said. 'I'm just trying this new skin care regime. I can't afford to break out in my line of work.'

'Oh. What do you do?' I asked.

'I'm trying to get into modelling.'

Trying? Odd. I would have thought he would be a shoo-in.

'Have you had any luck?'

'Bits and pieces. I've got a major shoot next week and I need to look perfect.'

You already are.

There was an anticipatory pause. What was he expecting me to say? I took a bite of my croissant, crumbs flying everywhere.

Maria came with his coffee and water. She put them down and stood waiting for I don't know what. The man returned to his phone. Maria sighed and left. She had it bad.

'Do you think a water reflection is truer than a mirror one?' he asked, not looking at me, but gazing in the glass. What an odd question.

'I've never thought about it.'

He put the glass onto my tray and said, 'Look. Tell me it isn't better.'

I wiped my mouth of crumbs and looked into the glass. All I saw was the white tray underneath. 'I can't see anything.'

He took the glass back. 'You're too used to using a mirror.'

He took out a brush and started brushing his hair, looking into the glass to style it at the front. How was he seeing anything in there?

I dreamt about the man for a few days, but his image vanished soon afterwards. I hadn't seen him in days, although I looked everywhere, and Maria hadn't either, or so she said. There was an odd look in her eyes when she shook her head at my question, which made me doubt her.

I was sitting on the stairs outside The River fountain-sculpture when I heard his voice.

'Do you think my skin is looking cleaner?'

Who was he talking to? I stopped reading The Encyclopaedia of Gods and looked up. The foliage prevented anyone from seeing around the sculpture.

'Never mind,' he continued, 'I definitely think it's cleaner. Here, touch it.' There was silence as I imagined someone touching him. 'I need to get some lenses to make my eyes bigger. The photographer at the last shoot said I had tiny eyes. What an idiot, right?'

'Right.' Maria.

I wasn't surprised, but why had she lied about not seeing him? Did she think I would be jealous? Or did she know she could never compete with me?

'What colour do you think I should get?' he asked her.

'Get clear ones. The colour can't be more perfect than it is already. You can't be more perfect than you are already.' Cringe. Had she really said that?

'That's true. Hold on. I just need to look at them again.' There were sounds but I couldn't make out what he was trying to do. 'The fountain's empty! What have they done to it?'

'It's gone?' Maria asked.

'But I was here last week and there was water here. I'm sure of it.'

'It's been leaking, the council website said. Maybe they drained it?'

'Oh, well. Thank the Lord for Birmingham's canals! Let's go!'

There were more sounds and then they left, arm in arm, watery reflections calling them.

That night I phoned Maria.
'Hey!' I said, all faux bouncy.
'Hey. How have you been?'
'Oh, you know. Keeping busy. You?'
'You know me.' Did I?
'I haven't seen you in ages! Do you want to grab a coffee together tomorrow?'
'Tomorrow? Erm, I've got two shifts at the café.'
'Oh, well, I can meet you there. You have a lunch break, right?'
'Right.'
Well, this conversation was going nowhere.
'Honestly, Maria, if you don't want to meet, just say so!'
There was silence, then a few throat clearings.
'So, erm, there's something I haven't told you. I'm er kind of er seeing someone.' It was all coming out now.
'Oh, my god, that's amazing! Who is he?' I didn't teach acting for nothing.
'He's erm. He's that man who sat with you, do you remember?'
'Oh, wow! Lucky you!'
'You don't mind?'
'Of course not!' I lied. 'What's he like?'
'Like an angel come to earth.' I heard the relief in her voice that I wasn't more upset. She wasn't wrong about the angel bit, though.
'So, you're actually spending the day with him tomorrow?'
'Tomorrow's our two-week anniversary, you see.' I internally snorted but I wasn't surprised. Maria had always been the sentimental type, even in school.

'Oh, congrats! How are you going to be spending it?'

'It's that exhibition tomorrow, do you remember, of the male statues? We'll go there in the morning, then grab some lunch somewhere.'

'Sounds divine! I'm very jealous!'

She laughed. 'Well, I'd better go. Have fun tomorrow! Bye!'

I spent the night on Birmingham Museum and Art Gallery's website.

Birmingham Museum and Art Gallery was bigger than people gave it credit for. So, it wasn't the British Museum, but then, what was? The exhibition didn't have a dedicated room: the statues were spread out all over, which was perfect for me.

I hid in the Gift Shop and watched them walk in. The very first statue was a Victorian replica of Hermes, but covered, as was their wont, those prudish Victorians. Would I know this burning if I had lived then?

Upon coming to the statue, the man stopped. I'd been too consumed to ask Maria what his name was, but what do names matter except in Shakespeare's plays?

The man and Maria took stock of the statue.

'Who's got the better face?' I heard him ask.

'Face?! You've got a better everything!'

'You're right. I am the most beautiful thing here.' Well. Someone was full of himself, wasn't he? And well he should be. 'Is there anywhere I can see my reflection?'

He was obsessed with his face, wasn't he?

Maria fumbled in her bag and handed him a mother-of-pearl backed mirror. He looked at his face and said, 'I can't even see all of my face in one go.'

'Go to the toilets. There'll be mirrors there.'

'Maybe. There'll also be water there! Let's go.'

Let's go?

Were they going together to the toilets? I quickly turned around, pretending to look at the giant painting of the sea, but I kept them in my sight. When they were ahead, I followed them to the newly installed gender-neutral toilets where they both entered.

I couldn't let them see me. They would know I was following them, and then what would happen?

I was admiring a modern copy of the statue of that boy in contrapposto. The statue was painted, which was quite common in Ancient Greece, but I didn't care. My senses were attuned to the man and Maria, but I heard them before I saw them.

'How can you think of lunch, Maria? Look at this spot on my nose! I only saw it because of the water reflection!'

Maria was silent. She wasn't the confrontational type, but this was a new development. Earlier, they had seemed bosom-bound; but this was a crack and where there were cracks...

I stood outside his house in Edgbaston. The way he talked and the products he used had given me an inkling that he was monied and this house in Edgbaston proved that. Detached, flowers everywhere, strung lights giving it a wealthy atmosphere, it looked far too big for one person. He clearly didn't do the modelling for the money.

He'd gone in a little while ago, all by himself.

What was he doing with Maria anyway? I was more like him; more beautiful, more confident than Maria. Was that why he was with her? Did he need her to say the kinds of things she had when I'd espied them at The River sculpture?

If he were with me, I would expend all my speech praising him.

Reflections

I knocked on his door. When he opened it, the embers in my bloodstream awakened and circulated, driving forth flames to all parts.

'Hi,' he said.

'Hi! I'm Maria's friend. We met at the café by the canal.'

'Oh, right, yes.'

In the silence, I drank him in.

He cocked his head. I held out a handkerchief to him.

'You dropped this at the museum. I called after you and Maria, but I don't think you heard me.'

'Oh.'

His 'Oh' was circular perfection.

'I told Maria and she gave me your address. I hope you don't mind?'

'Of course not.' He took the kerchief, opening it out, and rubbed his fingers across his monogram, stitched in gold.

I looked him over. His t-shirt showed off his muscles, as did his jeans. My gaze returned to his face. He was watching me.

Our gazes locked.

He held the door open and closed it behind me, his eyes never leaving mine. In the hall, a gigantic mirror took up a whole wall, and there were mirrors going up all the way up the stairs. He turned to the mirror.

'My nose needs surgery. What do you think?'

'No!' What was he thinking of? 'You mustn't let anyone near you with a knife.' We watched each other in the mirror. I saw the pleasure at my words.

'And my skin? Does it need more exfoliating?' He took off his t-shirt and allowed me to gaze upon marble. He took my hand and let it fly across his torso, leaving it to lie on his belt.

'Go ahead,' he said, and I did.

He stood before me, fervent flames flaring, flowing, overheating all my senses. He placed my hand on him and pushed me down. My breaths came and went and time didn't mean anything because such infallibility was in me.

When I returned, I discovered us draped on the stairs, he looking at himself in the mirrors, his golden hair mirrored in his golden skin, and his golden sheen mirrored in my mouth.

The mirror on his bedroom ceiling had a pewter frame, daffodils carved everywhere.

'Why daffodils?' I asked.

'They're my family's ancestral flower.'

'Ancestral flower?' I parroted. Was I turning into Maria? He nodded. 'That's a thing?'

'It's on our family's crest.'

His family had a crest. When I married him, would the crest be part of me?

In the reflection, he watched me lazily, a golden lion. My gaze didn't waver from his.

He sat up, on the edge of the bed and I sat at his feet.

'This is as it should be, isn't it?' he asked.

'Yes,' I said. 'Always like this.'

He leaned back until he fell onto the bed. My fingers, my tongue traced all, while he watched himself in the ceiling.

The bathwater was still as he leant over it. I stood in the doorway and wondered how this had all happened. What would I say to Maria? I would choose him over her, but a part of me wondered, nevertheless.

'Sit beside the tub and gaze at me,' he said.

Reflections

'Yes,' I replied.

'Maria,' I said, over the phone, 'I'm sorry.'
'Sorry? Why?'
'I'm in Edgbaston.' I said.
'Edgbaston? Why?'
'Why not?' There was no answer. 'I don't need to justify myself to you.'
'You're at his, aren't you?'
'Look, Maria, you were living in a dream. I'm not at his level. Who is? But you? You were to him as an atom is to the universe. Let him go and be happy.' A sob sounded, but I couldn't do anything, could I? After all, Lizzie Bennett was right when she told Lady Catherine de Burgh that she was determined to act in a way that would constitute her happiness, regardless of anyone else's feelings; and if you couldn't follow Lizzie Bennett's advice, whose could you?
'Be happy?' she said between sobs, her sounds turning contemplative.
'Yes.' I was no Libertarian, but my happiness was important, wasn't it?
'Yes.'

He didn't come to me that night so I searched for him near all the reflective surfaces of the house. I found him in the garden, on the edge of the pond, his dressing gown shining, its Far Eastern designs luminescing in the light of the moon.

He was still.

It scared me.

He looked up at me when I ran my fingers through his hair. I held out my hand to him, and led him to his bed, to what had rapidly become my bed. In my head, anyway.

I did wonder, though, at his feelings for me.

His gazing at me had lessened.
His gazing at himself had increased.

When the police told me he'd drowned in the canal, I didn't believe them. The universe wouldn't let his beauty die. Certainly not like that.

'There's CCTV from the café,' the policewoman said. 'It shows him looking into the canal for several hours before he fell in. Do you know what he might have been doing?'

I hung up.

Selfish man. He should have let me die looking upon his beauty, not him.

What would I do now?

I waited for him, long after he died, in the mirrors and waters and everywhere there were reflections, but his face never looked back at me.

DARK ANCHOR
By

Sam Spicer

SHAINA

'Hello?'

Shaina trembled, listened to the reply. It bounced through air; a globule of sound, bodiless and liberated; a breathy pinball drunkenly flung around walls, ceiling, floor. For a few moments it filled the space around her, vibrated every molecule. Then it fell into flat silence. The quiet settled heavy, adding its weight to the utter darkness; a darkness which now pressed closer, squeezing Shaina, stealing her oxygen, stroking her clammy skin with unseen terrors.

She opened her mouth to call out again, but what would be the point? The answer would be the same; her own tremulous voice echoing back. A taunt thrown out by the blackness.

She was alone.

Her hands were her eyes. She wafted them ahead of her, around her. Found a wall to her right. Felt the curve of the concrete, rough and grainy, yet slimy too. The instinct to recoil from the unpleasant sensation quashed by a greater need. The need to be guided. Haltingly, cautiously, her feet shuffled forward. Keeping one hand on the wall, the other danced before her face, probing, protecting.

The air in the tunnels was stale and sour. She hadn't noticed it when she had light. But that was ten minutes and several lifetimes ago. Now it was thick and oppressive, cruelly partnering with her own panic to make her skin hot, her breathing shallow. A bout of claustrophobia, something she'd never suffered from before, threatened, looming somewhere on the horizon.

All she could do was keep moving. And hope!

But hope was thin and slippery and kept sliding off to expose what lay beneath; a rock-solid wall of doom. Shaina wished the heat causing her to perspire would burn off some of the fear. She was sure if she could get her emotions under control she could think more rationally; use her wits to get out of here.

But perhaps not. Her own supposed cleverness had got her into this situation.

She'd recently volunteered to give tours of the tunnels. They were going to open them up to the public; at least for a limited time. Little known passageways ran beneath the streets of Birmingham. Hidden. Shaina had done the training. She'd learnt the history. Memorised the dates. But she'd been so focussed on the dry facts about the place that she'd omitted to learn all the details of the actual layout. She had a vague idea, but most of what she recalled were the various exit points, not the configuration of the passageways between them. It would be laughable if it weren't so tragic.

How could a day upend so spectacularly? She'd been so happy that morning. Felt so worthwhile, a part of something. After eighteen months of unemployment just the simple things about work had been fresh and exciting; wearing skirts and heels and makeup, instead of slouching around the flat in baggy t-shirts and leggings, scanning job vacancies on her phone, applying for positions with ever decreasing hope. The weight of the futility of her search bloating and growing and dragging her ever downward.

Then she'd been offered a place at a telecommunications company. Perhaps she should have been content with what was offered, kept it simple, head down, got on with her work, enjoyed the commute to the bustling city, relished occasional wine-fuelled lunches with colleagues, signed up for a few social events. But no, she'd had to start volunteering for anything that was going. She never wanted to return to the wasteland of joblessness, with its stale hours and empty days. She would prove her worth. Make herself, well, if not quite invaluable, at least desirable. Should the future bring job cuts her attitude, willingness and proactiveness would hopefully keep her afloat. The cream of the crop; less likely to be axed.

But if she'd limited herself she wouldn't be here now.

At first she'd thought her knowledge that these tunnels even existed had been a blessing. A way to escape the furious streets right now. But she'd only had a few training sessions. She knew some facts and figures, but it was all just stuff on paper. None of which prepared her for navigating through this labyrinth thirty-plus metres below the city.

If she'd just stuck to basics, she'd have been safely sitting at her desk right now. But she'd walked across town for one of the orientation sessions. As she was heading back trouble exploded all around her. She wasn't even sure what the protests were about. There'd been a couple of demonstrations in the last few days, peaceful for the most part. She'd been vaguely aware of trouble flaring up a few nights ago, but that had spilled out of the pubs at some late hour. But it seemed a bigger pot of discontent had been ready to boil over. And she'd been right at ground zero when it happened.

Still plumped up with pride at her latest achievement, she'd sauntered around a corner smack bang into a street crammed with protesters. She'd come to a standstill, considering her options. Too eager to get back to the office, not wanting to turn around, find another way, go a longer way around, she'd stupidly opted to squeeze her way through the throng. At first it was just uncomfortable, unnerving, being jostled, elbowed, shoved this way and that as she squashed her way through all the bodies. Then the energy in the crowd changed. Gaps opened up. The gathering loosened. But this wasn't a good thing. It turned from a group of protesters to an angry mob in a matter of seconds. Shaina had no clue what sparked the transformation, but she was in the heart of it. Voices yelled, screamed out of angry mouths. Fists were brandished, punches thrown. Projectiles started flying. Where the rocks came from she couldn't comprehend. Soon there was screaming and the sounds of glass smashing. Shaina, hands over her head, bent low, cowered amongst the chaos. She tried to flee, but there seemed no safe direction. Every way she turned there were eyes filled with hatred, casting about for targets.

She found a wall, stuck to it, just to feel something solid at her back, but she was still exposed, vulnerable. A bottle shattered inches from her. She felt the sting of shards as the glass exploded. Spots of blood on her cheek. She sobbed, looking around hopelessly.

That's when she'd seen it. The tell-tale tower rising up. One of the vents. A door would be on the other side: a secret door to a secret world. And she had the key. She was scheduled to do a training tour that weekend. The instructor had given out a couple of sets of keys and she'd been one of the lucky ones. Suddenly there was a glimmer of hope, a way to escape. She just had to get to it.

She'd run, clumsy in heels, dodging and weaving. She was almost through when she was pulled up short; found herself staring into a hideous face. It wasn't the features themselves, but the deranged ferocity. The feral violence pulsing just below the skin. He gripped her arm, yanking her backwards. Shaina screamed and lashed out.

Her new nails helped. She slashed and clawed until his grasp loosened. The moment she could she jerked her arm free and ran as fast as she could. She heard loud footsteps behind. Not just one set either. She risked a glance over her shoulder. Her attacker had friends. A small voice wondered 'Why me?' but a louder one overrode it. Fighting was happening all around. It didn't matter who you were, just that you were there. The violence itself had taken over, and it didn't care about what was rational or reasonable; it was just hungry for more. Shaina had an escape plan and she had the key, but she needed time to fish it out from the depths of her handbag. Then more time, to get the door open, lock it behind her.

She knew right now she didn't have that window of time available to her. So, hating that this was the only choice, she turned sharply, heading straight back into the roiling mob. It worked. She was buffeted from every side, but no-one else was targeting her directly. Not yet anyway. But the riot seemed to be growing, no sign of things quietening down. At least she'd lost her crazed attackers in the crowd. Crouching and weaving she carefully reached into her bag and found the key. She grasped it in her fist as if her life depended on it - which it very well might. Once she thought it was reasonably safe, she tried again, running for the ventilation tower. This time there were no sounds of pursuit.

She climbed a short metal ladder, up and over, disappeared from the view of the horde. She might have waited there, in a dusty abandoned yard, but then she heard the rattle of the ladder. In a trice she'd let herself in through the door. Quickly locked it behind her. When the handle rattled she'd gasped, stepping away from the door. The door was sturdy. It was locked. But she still feared they – whoever they were – might get in. Her fear had followed her into the tunnels. She didn't wait around. Just in case, she'd moved on. Her phone gave her light. She would find another exit.

Such a simple idea.

Now she was lost. Her light had gone. The battery on her phone quickly dwindled and died. All she had left was fear, confusion and darkness.

At least things couldn't get any worse.

But then they did.

At first she thought it was the rats again. Their scuttling in the pitch black had been a frequent soundtrack as she'd stumbled her way deeper into the tunnels. The sounds seemed to come from one direction then bounce around. She couldn't be sure where they came from, or how far away they were. All she knew was that every time the scampering and scratching reached her ears it made her skin pucker and crawl with fear and revulsion.

This time there was something different about the noise. It didn't match the earlier scurrying. Instead she heard tapping, regular, almost rhythmic. She paused, standing still to listen. This warren of concrete passageways was mischievous though, ricocheting and echoing and fooling her ears. The sound was real. But she had no idea what was making it, or what direction it was coming from.

Shaina started moving again. She'd been going for a while. She had a vague notion of another exit and hoped she was getting closer. How she'd know when she was close, she wasn't sure. What she'd give for a torch. A match. Any scrap of light! But she had none so would just have to make do.

She tried to speed up, unnerved by the ceaseless tap tap tap that seemed now to follow her. She'd got used to walking without seeing, comforted and guided by the wall that she kept one hand sliding over. She just hoped she didn't encounter any obstacles. The instructor in her training said the upper tunnels had been cleared of equipment and she sincerely hoped that was true. A leftover box or reel of cable could send her plunging headlong. She had enough to contend with. She didn't want to add an injury into the mix.

Suddenly the wall she'd been following vanished. Shaina stopped dead. Turned. Both hands now flailing she felt around desperately. She backtracked a few steps, found the wall again. The air felt different too. Very slightly. She realised the wall had vanished because there was another opening there on her right. She'd either reached a junction or the tunnel turned a corner. She tried to think back to the slideshow in her training. The pictures of the passageways. Their configuration. But she couldn't remember clearly. Couldn't place where she was. She thought she should keep going straight if that were possible. That was the best way not to get hopelessly lost. If she didn't come across another way out, if she really had to, she could at least turn around and go back the way she'd come. She took a deep breath. Both hands out in front of her she groped blindly, stepping out into space. She felt dizzy with disorientation. As she carefully crept forward, her ears focussed in again on the sound. The tapping. It was louder now. It was clearer. There was something else too. Another sound beneath. A slow, muffled shuffling followed the sharper raps. Shaina again came to a complete halt. She froze. Her fear ramped up to terror as she realised two things. The first was that the sound was getting closer because it was ahead of her. She was heading right for it. The second thing she realised was that the fainter, shuffling noise was in fact footsteps.

She wasn't alone down here.

Heart thumping, breath stalling, she felt faint, clammy. She had to try and get a grip. She turned, listening to be sure. Turned again. In her panic she was behaving erratically. She was adrift. Which way had she come? She needed to head back. Someone else was down here. She thought about the man who'd tried to attack her. The violence erupting on the streets. Had one of the troublemakers found their way in here too?

Shaina no longer knew which way was which. But the sound was getting ever closer. She rotated, again and again, slowly, ears pricked. She had to be sure in which direction the danger lay before she moved.

'Hello.'

She gasped. This time the voice floating through the tunnels wasn't her own echo. It was someone else. A deep, raspy voice. A man. That voice in the dark was horrific, the realisation of a nightmare. Here she was, a trapped animal, pursued, hunted. There was only one crumb of comfort. She was fairly sure now she had a bearing on where he was. So she hurried away in the opposite direction. She collided with a wall, jolting her shoulder painfully. She tried to bite back the cry on her lips. But it didn't matter. He'd heard her already. Her stupid heels pinging like sonar for him to follow. She removed them. Barefoot, she fled.

HENRY

He paused to catch his breath, one hand steadying himself against the wall. The place smelt damp now. Musty and dank. Very different from all those years ago. Then, the air was alive with the scent of fresh concrete; a fine dust pervaded everything. So dry. The only moisture back then the sweat beneath his shirt as he'd darted about the tunnels. He briefly mourned the boy he'd once been. That youngster didn't tire so quickly. A teenager back then he'd lacked experience, skills, but had energy. They found plenty of use for him. Running with messages, carrying equipment, doing the heavy lifting. The work was tough, but he'd thrived on the challenge. The secrecy added extra spice. Nobody was supposed to know about the tunnel system being dug out

Dark Anchor

far below the city centre. Its true purpose? An underground telephone exchange built to withstand nuclear attack. He'd been sworn to silence. They all had.

A lot had changed in the decades between then and now. Henry himself had changed dramatically. He was old now. Scampering about was a mere whiff of a memory, drifting away on the intervening years. His body had slowed, thickened, stooped. Time pressed on him, coiled around him, coated him in weariness, weakness. Then there were the afflictions; the sugar coating of old age. Arthritis, stiff and swollen joints. If all of that weren't enough to burden him, twelve years ago he'd lost his sight.

Henry pushed back away from the wall. Stood upright, gripped his cane, and set off again. His body betrayed him at every turn, but his mind was as sharp as ever.

As he set off again he wondered why she'd ventured so far from the door. Probably fear. The streets were no place to be today. That's why he had ventured inside. To avoid the riots that had broken out above. He knew the secret ways in; knew his way around. Even all these years later.

He was lucky. Despite his advancing years his hearing, unlike his sight, had never declined. It was as sharp as ever - as was his memory. He remembered now how sounds down here would gambol about, try to fool you with echoes that ricocheted in all directions. But as a lad he'd soon got used to that. When the tunnels were under construction the men and machines clamoured and clattered and screeched all day long. His name was called a lot; summoning him to the next task. He was always in demand. So young, so quick, so eager. He'd quickly learned to distinguish the direction of the summons. Yes, in the beginning the mischievous caverns had led him merrily down the wrong passageway. But he got wise to it soon enough. He learned to navigate not only the labyrinth of new tunnels they were creating, but also the peculiarities of the sound waves down here.

It all came back so naturally - even though back then, he'd still had the use of his eyes. Henry quietly admitted to himself that his blindness probably enhanced his interpretation of the noises he heard.

Footsteps retreating, heels clattering rapidly against concrete. A flurry of erratic speed; stumbling and disjointed. Then it stopped, briefly. When the footsteps started up again, they were quiet, a soft flapping now, so much softer than the sharp tapping of a moment ago. But still retreating. Still getting further away. Why was she running from him?

'No, wait!' he called, but his appeal floated impotently in the wake of her flight. Henry sighed, resting again for a moment against the wall. He could do with a sit down. It crossed his mind to leave. He was in good shape for his age, but certainly not up to running about down here like a scuttling mole in its burrow. He was getting tired, and thirsty. The air down here was heavy and humid, laced with a damp odour that cloyed at the back of his throat. He knew about the flooding in some areas. Hopefully he wouldn't come across any today. Again he pondered leaving. He could alert the authorities that someone was lost in the tunnels. He assumed she was lost. His sharp ears had been tuned in to her for some time, gauging her distance, her direction. His memory filling in the details, examining the route she had taken. There was no logic to the path she'd chosen. She seemed to be merely stumbling erratically. Now she'd dashed off on a totally new tangent, startled he realised by his presence.

Henry straightened up, took a couple of gulps of stale air, then moved on. Following the faint sound of her rapidly fleeing footsteps. He recognised the junction; knew the way she was going wouldn't lead to a way out. He had to help her, even if she was being silly right now. If he could get close enough, he knew he could reassure her. He just needed to explain who he was, and that he knew where the nearest exit was. She'd be grateful. He could do something good today. Help someone. He could rest later.

Henry's tired legs kept going. His mind drifted. The boy he'd been had scarpered around this underground warren with ease; nimble and tireless. Now he carried the burden of years and they dragged at him. But being here again did cause those memories to resurface. He'd forgotten so much: the laughter of workmen resonating, the clang of tools, the whiff of cigarette smoke mingled with concrete. Despite the sapping fatigue he was glad to walk these halls again, to reclaim those lost images, recall the vigour and activity of the place – or, indeed, remember the vigour and activity of the keen, youthful fellow he'd been. He smiled to himself. He'd make one last dash through the Anchor tunnels. Well, doddering shuffle was more like it. But still, he felt the ghost of his youth at his side and was glad of the company.

The tunnels had been named Anchor because they passed under the Assay Office in the city, and the hallmark symbol for Birmingham was the anchor. He paused to get his bearings, remembering how many steps he'd taken since the last junction, letting his ears attune to this stretch of passageway. He wasn't beneath the Assay Office now though; they were getting off track. She'd run off in the worst direction if they were to find a quick and easy way to get back to street level. Henry sighed and cocked his head.

There. A rustle up ahead. He was slowly gaining on her. She was agile and swift, so why was he gaining? Yes, he was familiar with the layout down here. But he was old and slow. Perhaps she was hurt.

He considered calling out again. He was gaining but still not as close as he'd like. He knew how sounds were distorted, especially from a distance. Shouting now might have her scuttling in another direction. Also his voice might be garbled, and he wanted to reassure her. No, he'd see if he could make up a bit more ground first.

Tapping his cane ahead of him to feel for obstacles, Henry set off again.

SHAINA

There it was again, that tap, tap, tap. It haunted her. The slow, rhythmic, unyielding persistence of the sound. Following her everywhere she went. So dull a sound, but it sent threads of terror weaving through her. She carried her shoes now. Hoping for quiet steps in her bare feet. But the ground was so hard that the soles of her feet were becoming tender, not to mention cold. How did he know which way she was going? She'd tried to be so quiet. And she'd seen no source of light at all. At times he sounded close, but there was no torch beam cutting through the dark. The blackness of the tunnels was complete and unending. She began to cry. Desperate, hopeless tears cooling on her cheeks. Her imagination was taking flight. This man, able to find his way without light, able to track her when she was so silent, was being transformed into something more sinister: some supernatural, subterranean, dark-dwelling creature that lurked and hunted beneath the city. Maybe not even that. Maybe not a monster, but a ghost. Some spectral being that stalked these hallways, seeking the living to terrify and... and what? What would he/it do to her when it caught up?

She felt sure it would get her in the end. No matter how stealthy she was, how swift, how cunning, it just kept coming.

Shaina was desperate to get away, but her feet faltered to a halt. For a moment she was overcome with such hopelessness that it seemed blacker and denser than the darkness surrounding her.

Then she became aware of the shoes she carried in her hands. Her high heels.

She wasn't entirely helpless.

If the thing that pursued her had flesh and bones maybe she could hurt it. If it was just a man, maybe she should stand and fight. Running was getting her nowhere. Literally. Doing her best to shake off her tears and terror, Shaina turned around, now facing the way she'd come, and she waited.

HENRY

He could no longer hear her. The flurry of soft footsteps, the flustered gasps, they'd evaporated. For a moment Henry doubted his senses. Had he imagined her? He set his jaw and shook off any such misgivings. He was as bright as ever and his quick ears hadn't failed him yet. He kept going, doggedly putting one foot in front of the other, his cane arcing out before him, checking the terrain, feeling for obstacles. Henry would find the lost woman. The quiet was unnerving. He feared she'd come to harm. Perhaps she'd fallen? Hurt herself? Or just stopped running through weariness. He was certainly weary, even at this sedate pace. It occurred to him he could pass right by her. If she'd passed out he might miss her. Walk by and never realise it. He slowed a little, taking tiny steps, straining his ears further for any little clue as to her whereabouts.

When he finally heard a sound it was right behind him.

He started to turn, flooded with relief. 'Ah, there you…'

The blow stung and shocked. So much so he felt the world tilt. He was floating, dazed, sparks of pain shooting along the side of his head. Then another blow - no, a collision - his body hitting the ground. His cane clattered away. He flailed, groaned, cried out. 'Please, no!' He should defend himself, try to move, to get up, or crawl away, but the attack had rendered him immobile. He managed to raise his arms, pull them up over his head. He felt the sticky sensation over his ear, probed the wound. The pain of it caused him to groan again. Henry's body wasn't cooperating yet, but his mind, his voice, could still function.

'Why are you doing this?' he asked. 'I was just trying to help. Why did you attack me?'

He knew she was there. Close. He could hear the ragged breathing. He could smell her; sweetly perfumed sweat laced with fear. It hadn't occurred to him that she might be dangerous. He felt a little strength return to his limbs, began dragging himself away. 'Please, just let me go.'

SHAINA

There was no monster. There was no ghoul. There was no rabid attacker hunting her in the dark.

There was an old man. Lying at her feet. Injured and pleading.

But perhaps there was a monster after all, and its name was Shaina.

'Oh God, I'm so sorry.' She reached down; her fingers connected with the fabric of his coat. She felt him flinch. 'I thought... I mean, there was trouble out there. I thought you were one of them.'

He was moving feebly, trying to inch away from her. She couldn't blame him.

'I really am sorry. I honestly thought I was in danger. You were following me.'

For a few moments she heard nothing but his raspy breath and meagre attempts to get away from her. Then, 'I thought you were lost. I wanted to help. To show you the way out.'

'But how did you find me? It's pitch dark in here.'

'I'm blind,' he told her. 'I find my way in the dark every day.' His voice was shaky. Weak.

'Please, let me help you.' Without waiting for assent, she knelt down, felt for his arm, helped him sit up. 'Do you think you can stand?'

'Not yet,' he said. 'I'm dizzy.'

'Oh, right. Did I hurt you badly?'

'My head…'

Shaina was filled with shame and frustration. She had to make amends. 'What can I do? I can't even take a look down here.'

She heard him rummaging, then a small rattling sound. He found her wrist, her hand, placed something in it. She felt the small rectangular cardboard box, shook it. Matches. Shaina quickly lit one, finally getting a look at the man she'd feared, then attacked.

She guessed he was in his eighties, slightly built, a ruffled halo of downy grey hair framing his features. The eyes stared ahead, unaffected by the flicker of the tiny flame she'd struck. She peered at the side of his head. A nasty gash leached blood into his sparse silver hair. She'd hurt him but hopefully hadn't done too much damage.

'Here, I have a scarf in my bag. Let me put it round your head.' He sat, compliant, as she wrapped the wound. 'It doesn't look too deep,' she told him. The match that she'd put on the floor whilst she tended him quickly went out. Shaina sat next to the man, gripping the little box.

'Lucky you had these.' She rattled the match box.

'For my pipe,' he said. 'Thank goodness for bad habits, eh?'

'What's your name?'

'Henry.'

'I'm Shaina.'

He merely sighed. They stayed there in silence for a while. Finally, 'You said something about showing me the way out. How can you find your way? I mean… I just mean I've struggled to find my way and I've had training about these tunnels.'

For several long seconds he didn't reply. Shaina began to fear he'd passed out. Or worse.

'I helped build them,' he eventually said. 'Back in the fifties, I worked down here. Remember every twist and turn.'

Shaina realised her luck had changed. She now had a guide and a source of light. Though there weren't many matches in the little box that she clung to so eagerly. 'How about we get out of here,' she said, struggling to her feet. 'You know the way out, right?'

'Oh yes,' Henry's voice was faint in the darkness. 'In a moment,' he mumbled. 'Just need to rest for a while.'

Shaina stood there, waiting, listening to the silence as it deepened around her, the black air becoming still and empty.

'Hello?'

Birmingham Writers' Group

Birmingham Writers' Group was founded in 1946 and is a space where writers of all experience, abilities and interests can meet to share their work and hone their craft. We have members who are traditionally published, self-published, unpublished, and everything in between.

Although all the works in this collection are short stories, we encourage submissions of all kinds of writing, from prose novels to poems and articles.

In ordinary times, we meet twice monthly in the Deritend Room in Saint Martin's in the Bull Ring. However, 2020 has been a challenging year for all of us, and Birmingham Writers' Group is no exception. In March, we made the difficult decision to end our face-to-face meetings and moved to virtual meetings. At the time of writing this introduction, the Covid-19 pandemic is hitting its 'second wave' and so, for the foreseeable future, our meetings will continue to be held virtually.

Whether our meetings are in person or held virtually, we always welcome new members. If you are interested in attending our next meeting, please go to our website and click on our 'How to Join' section.

http://www.birminghamwriters.org/

ABOUT THE AUTHORS

ALISON THERESA GIBSON grew up in Canberra, the illusive capital of Australia, and currently lives in Birmingham, UK. She has words in a number of publications, including *Spelk*, *Litro*, *Crack the Spine*, *Meanjin*, and *Every Day Fiction*, and she won the *Furious Gazelle* Spring Writing Contest in June 2019. She is currently completing her MA in Creative Writing at University of Birmingham. Find her @byAlisonTheresa and alisontheresa.com.

SIMON FAIRBANKS is the author of the Nephos novels, an ongoing fantasy series, currently consisting of *The Sheriff* and *The Curse of Besti Bori*. He has written three short story collections, *Breadcrumbs*, *Boomsticks* and *Belljars*, each containing a novella set within his Nephos fantasy world. Simon is also the author of Treat or Trick, a multiple-pathway novel, with twenty-six different endings. He has been a member of the Birmingham Writer's Group since 2011. His website is www.simonfairbanks.com.

I ROBIN IRIE grew up in Jamaica and writes stories that draw on this rich culture. His interest in history causes him to mine the past for inspiration. He is currently seeking an agent for his first novel, an epic fantasy with an African setting. A husband and a father, he spends his days masquerading as an accountant, which is totally congruous with being a writer of fiction. He is also a long-suffering fan of Arsenal Football Club.

ABOUT THE AUTHORS

JANE ANDREWS grew up in the north of England and moved to Birmingham to study for a BA in English Literature and French in 1985. Since then, she has lived in many different parts of the country, and now teaches English in a school in Birmingham. She is the author of the *Sarah and Steve* YA trilogy, the *Dreamworld* YA fantasy series, two novels set in Birmingham in the 1980s (*Full Circle* and *A Degree of love*) and two chick-lit novels (*A Perfect Arrangement* and *Shopping For Love*) as well as having short stories published in two anthologies by the Didcot Writers' Group and two by the Australian company *Pure Slush*. She has also previously published the short story '*Hope in the City*' in BWG's *City of Hope* anthology.

CHRIS MURTAGH is probably the finest writer of the twenty-first century not to win the Nobel prize, according to Chris. Check out murta_chris on Instagram.

HAZEL WARD is a writer, poet and occasional blogger. Several of her short stories have been published in anthologies and online. The publication of her debut novel, *The Three Things That Broke Netta Wilde* is getting ever closer. In the meantime, she is working on the sequel, as well as a novella and a collection of stories and poems based on her early life in the back to backs of inner-city Birmingham. Follow her on Twitter, Instagram or at https://hazelward.wordpress.com. You can also see her performing her poetry on her YouTube channel.

ABOUT THE AUTHORS

C.P. GARGHAN began writing on his grandmother's typewriter. Though the technology might have changed, his love for inventive stories hasn't. His stories range from the eerie to the hopeful. He has previously been published in *City of Night: An Anthology of Birmingham Stories*, and *City of Hope*, both celebrations of his home city
In 2020, he self-published *The Mapmaker Moths*, his first collection of short stories
When he isn't writing short stories, Christopher is working on longer works, several of which are seeking representation from publishers.

KIRSTY HANDLEY came to Birmingham for University and has never left after being captivated by the city. She writes flash fiction and short stories usually with a dystopian theme and is delighted to feature in this anthology. Her story Ice featured in the 2020 Flash Fiction journal. She graduated with a degree in Business Management and enjoys writing as an outlet to unleash some creativity.

R L PARKINSON lives in Birmingham with her partner. She began her writing career with various short stories, where the past influences the present, touching on nostalgia and memories. She is also working on a series of short stories for children. When not writing or working in her full-time job in healthcare administration, she spends valuable time with her family and likes to put her hand to a variety of crafts and creative projects.

ABOUT THE AUTHORS

MOHAMMED RIZWAN is mostly a flash fiction writer who occasionally dabbles in longer forms. He is currently writing two novels.

SAM SPICER grew up in the West Midlands of England, where she still lives. An avid and enthusiastic reader from childhood she now indulges her passion for writing. Sam is the author of the Edward Gamble Mystery novels (*The Art of Detection, Canvassing Crime and The Mystery Artist*), and of the Blackbridge crime series (*Fallout, Sweet Murder and Cold Fury*). She has also previously published the short story *Star Gazer* (as J. S. Spicer) in the *City of Night* anthology.